OFF THE RECORD

A WITH ME IN SEATTLE MAFIA NOVEL

KRISTEN PROBY

AMPERSAND PUBLISHING, INC.

Off the Record
A With Me In Seattle MAFIA Novel
By

Kristen Proby

OFF THE RECORD

A With Me In Seattle MAFIA Novel

Kristen Proby

Copyright © 2021 by Kristen Proby

All Rights Reserved. This book may not be reproduced, scanned, or distributed in any printed or electronic form without permission from the author. Please do not participate in or encourage piracy of copyrighted materials in violation of the author's rights. All characters and storylines are the property of the author and your support and respect are appreciated. The characters and events portrayed in this book are fictitious. Any similarity to real persons, living or dead, is coincidental and not intended by the author.

Cover Design: By Hang Le

Cover photo: Wander Aguiar

Paperback ISBN: 978-1-63350-085-3

For Chelle.
Thank you, for everything.
I couldn't do this without you.

PROLOGUE

~ANNIKA~

*R*afe Martinelli. Also known as the love of my life. The man of my dreams. My one and only. I know, I'm only twenty, and my cousin Nadia would tell me that it's completely ridiculous to think that I could meet my soul mate in college when I should be out sowing my wild oats—whatever in the world that means.

I love Nadia. She's my closest friend, as well as my cousin, and she's one of a very select few who knows what it's like to live in this crazy family of ours. My roommate, Ivie, knows.

And Rafe.

Because while my uncle is the boss of one of the most prominent crime families in the country, Rafe's father is the boss of *the* biggest family on the west coast.

And our families don't like each other.

Which means that everything Rafe and I are to each other, everything we've done, and what we're about to do tonight is a secret.

Because if our families found out, we'd be in big trouble.

"Class dismissed."

I sigh in relief when my biology professor gives us the okay to leave. I gather my books and papers and rush out of the lab toward my car.

Ivie and I live in an apartment just on the edge of campus. My uncle is kind enough to pay for it. Lord knows, neither Ivie nor I could afford it.

I know, I'm a lucky girl.

My date with Rafe is in an hour. Which means, I have to take a shower and get ready to go fast because Rafe is never late.

It's just one of the million reasons I love him so much.

"Hi, friend," I announce as I rush past Ivie to my bedroom. "Can't talk. Gotta hurry."

"I'll follow you," she says and leans her shoulder against the door of my bedroom as I strip naked and make a beeline for the bathroom. "What lit a fire under your butt?"

"Date."

"With Rafe?"

"It'd better be with Rafe. He'd be pretty mad if it was with someone else."

Ivie smirks as I start the shower and throw my hair

up under a shower cap. She's the only one who knows about Rafe and me. I *had* to tell her. She lives here, and I spend a lot of time with him.

"Tonight's the night," I inform her.

"Of what? Is there a new movie out?"

"No, it's *the* night."

She flings the shower curtain back and stares at me with wide, blue eyes. "You're going to *do it?*"

"Yep." I smile and shave one armpit. "I've been on the pill for a month, so we're covered there. I mean, we've literally done *everything* else. It's borderline torture. I'm so ready. He does things to me that I didn't even know were possible. The way I feel when he looks at me, let alone what happens to my skin, to my stomach when he touches me... I'm telling you, Ivie, it's incredible."

"I'm totally jealous." She pulls the curtain shut again, but I can hear her organizing things on the countertop. "Also, you're stupidly hot together. Like, you could be a celebrity couple, you're so pretty. It's like Brangelina."

I lather up one leg but pull the curtain aside so I can grin at my best friend. "You're so sweet. Thank you."

"I think you should tell your parents."

"No." I get to work shaving and shake my head, even though she can't see me. "No way. Uncle Igor would throw a fit, and I'd be in big trouble. I don't even want to think about what the punishment for this would be. And for Rafe, it would be worse. So, no. It's our secret."

"But what happens after this, Annika? I know it's exciting now, but you won't be in college forever. What then? Are you going to get married in secret and have secret babies?"

Tears want to threaten, but I swallow them and rinse my legs.

"Stop it. Tonight is going to be special, and I'm not going to think about the future and ruin it. It'll all work out. All I can do is live day to day."

I wrap the towel around me and immediately reach for my makeup bag.

"I don't agree with you, but I hope tonight is everything you want it to be." She pats me on the shoulder and leaves the bathroom, and I stare at my reflection.

"Everything's going to be just fine."

"Are you okay?"

"You've asked me that about six times." I smile at Rafe as he tucks a loose strand of hair behind my ear. The truth is, I'm sore, and it hurt way more than I thought it would, and was over pretty fast, too. But I've also never felt more connected to a person in my life as I do right now, lying in Rafe's giant bed.

"Are *you* okay?" I ask him and drag my fingertip down his nose. Rafe is a handsome man. He's tall and broad, and I know he works out almost every day. The efforts show. He has muscles on top of muscles and tanned skin. I could lick every inch of him.

And have.

"I don't think I've ever been better." His smile is soft, lazy, and a little proud. "You're amazing, babe."

I grin and rest my head on his shoulder. When I draw circles on his chest, he clasps my hand in his, kisses it, then holds it against his heart.

"I wish we could just stay right here, forever," I whisper.

"Me, too."

"What do you think will happen?"

He sighs. He knows exactly what I'm talking about.

"I don't mean to ruin this night," I rush on. "Forget I said anything."

"You didn't ruin anything," he assures me and kisses my forehead. "And the honest answer is, I don't know."

"We're meant to be together," I continue. "I mean, how else do you explain that we randomly chose the same college? And on the east coast, no less? This isn't a fluke. It's destiny. Maybe we can convince our families of that. Eventually."

"Maybe." He kisses my forehead again. "Eventually."

~

Two years later...

. . .

I've been summoned to my uncle's office. I don't quite know what to make of that, given that it's never happened before.

I smile at his assistant, who nods and says, "You can go on in, Annika."

"Thanks."

I push through the milky glass doors and am surprised to see not only Uncle Igor but also my father.

"Close the door, please," Uncle Igor says. He's sitting behind his enormous desk, looking more powerful than any man I've ever seen.

But he's never frightened me. He's always been loving and generous with me.

"Is something wrong?" I ask as I sit in the chair across from my uncle, next to my father.

"No. Actually, we have some good news for you. But first, I want to congratulate you on doing so well in college, my little firefly." Uncle Igor smiles proudly. "You finished your bachelors in just three years, and you're on track to finish medical school in only two years."

"That's right. And I want to thank *you* for the opportunity. I know it's not inexpensive, and I appreciate everything the family has done for me."

"I know you do. You're a good girl, Annika." Uncle Igor and my father share a look. "I wanted to let you know that you'll be moving to Denver for your residency."

I frown and shake my head. "I don't understand."

"You'll be switching schools in the fall. You'll complete your residency in Denver."

What about Rafe?

"Why? I'm doing well here, and I like this college. I have friends here."

"I know." He folds his hands on his desk. "And a boyfriend, eh?"

I blink rapidly. I *hate* lying to my family. "No, of course, not."

He tosses several photos on the desk in front of me, and I swallow hard when I see images of Rafe and me, walking hand-in-hand on campus, laughing while seated at our favorite restaurant, and kissing on a bridge where we like to take walks.

"You've never been a liar before, firefly."

I feel my father shift next to me, and tears immediately threaten.

"I don't like lying now," I confess and swallow hard.

"You know that the Martinellis are off-limits."

I clasp my hands tightly in my lap.

"Look at me," he says, but his voice is gentle, and his eyes hold compassion when I meet his. "You fancy yourself in love, do you?"

"Yes."

He nods and turns to look out the windows.

"He was sent here to follow you."

I blink, certain I've heard him wrong.

"They're keeping an eye on you and trying to get

information. The fact that they'd stoop so low and use my innocent niece as a pawn is unforgivable."

"No, that's not what's happening. Rafe was surprised to see me. We didn't know we were attending the same college."

"Annika," Papa says beside me and reaches for my hand. "You know this is not possible. It's forbidden."

A tear drops onto my cheek. "I didn't mean to fall in love with him any more than I can be to blame for his family tree."

"You're smarter than this," Uncle Igor says. "And I'm ending it. Now. Your last day of class is Friday. You'll be packed up and moved by Saturday afternoon. I've already arranged for the movers. This is not up for discussion."

My world is crumbling out from under me.

"What about Ivie?"

"She'll go with you. I know she's your closest friend and your confidante. I'm not a monster."

I have to try. I have to fight for what Rafe and I have. "Please, Uncle Igor. If you could just listen. If you could maybe talk to Rafe..."

"I am not at fault here," he replies, his voice hard now. "You know what it means to be a part of this family. You *know* that the Martinellis are off-limits. You need to remember your place and be grateful that simply changing schools is your punishment for defying me."

He's all boss now. I know better than to talk back.

So, I simply nod.

"Yes, sir."

"Good. End it today. I have an apartment waiting for you and Ivie in Denver. It's in a nice part of town and is newer than the place you have here."

"Thank you." It's a whisper.

When they dismiss me, I walk on numb legs out of the office building and stand on the sidewalk in the sunshine.

My God, how will I tell him?

CHAPTER 1

~RAFE~

Present Day

"They *met* with him?" I demand. I shove my hands into the pockets of my tux and work at keeping my face expressionless.

We're at a wedding, for Christ's sake.

"Pop confirmed it last night," Carmine says, rocking back on his heels. "I meant to pull you both in and tell you, but things got crazy."

"It was the night before your wedding," Shane reminds him. "Of course, it's crazy. What in the hell were they thinking, going in there alone? They're too old for that shit."

I share a look with my brothers, and then we all chuckle.

"They may be older," I reply, speaking of our father and Carmine's new father-in-law, Igor Tarenkov, both bosses of two of the strongest crime families in the world, "but they're not weak. They're also smart. If they went in to talk to those in Carlito's office without us, they knew what they were doing."

"Yeah, well," Carmine says, "I wish they'd let us in on it."

"This isn't the time or place," Shane says and claps a hand on our eldest brother's shoulder. "We're here to celebrate. Go dance with your bride. I'm going to find my smokin' hot fiancée and take her for a spin around the dance floor myself. Did you see how hot she looks today?"

Carmine and I smile as Shane hurries off to find Ivie.

"She's good for him," I say, watching as our brother takes Ivie's hand, kisses it, and then pulls her onto the dance floor. "She makes him happy."

"She does." Carmine nods and then glances to our left, motioning with his head. "She seems to frustrate you."

I follow his gaze and sigh when my eyes land on Annika. My gut churns, the way it always does whenever I see the woman I've loved for almost a decade.

"She does more than that," I murmur and sip my champagne. "I want to kiss the fuck out of her and take her over my damn knee."

Carmine laughs and taps his glass to mine. "That's a

woman for you. I think I'll follow our brother's lead and go find my wife."

His grin flashes over his face.

"My wife."

"You went and chained yourself to a dame for the rest of your life."

"Hell, yes. And I'd do it again in a heartbeat if it meant I could marry Nadia all over again."

"I guess you're allowed to be sappy on your wedding day. Go find your bride and dance inappropriately for a while."

"My pleasure."

Carmine saunters across the room, his eyes set on Nadia. She's a beautiful bride, and her eyes light up when she turns to see Carmine approaching.

They're both a couple of saps.

I guess I would be, too. I turn to look at Annika once more and sigh. She's as stunning as ever, with her long, blond hair falling around her in loose curls. Her makeup is flawless and more glammed-up for the occasion. The dress she's in showcases every curve to perfection, and my fingers ache with my desire to touch her.

Hell, it's not just my fingers that ache.

I've become accustomed to admiring her from afar. Keeping my distance.

Giving her space.

But my patience is running thin.

Her piece-of-shit husband has been dead for months. Nothing's standing in our way now.

Nothing except her stubbornness.

I set my empty glass on a tray and walk to where Annika is sitting, alone. She's holding an envelope, and I watch as she tears it open, quickly pages through the contents, and then runs a shaking hand through that silky hair.

I'm not at all ashamed that I look over her shoulder.

I almost wish I hadn't.

The image in her hands has my blood running cold.

"What the fuck is that?"

She jumps, puts the photo face-down on the table, and turns to me. "Oh, you startled me. It's nothing."

"I'll put up with a lot of things from you, Annika, but lying isn't one of them." I lean down, leveling my gaze with hers. "What is that?"

She swallows hard, glances down, and shoves everything back into the envelope. "Not now. Not here. It's Nadia's special day, and I won't ruin it with this. Especially not with this."

She turns embarrassed eyes up to me.

"Annika."

"Let's dance." She shoves the envelope into a bag under the table, takes my hand, and tries to pull me onto the dance floor.

But I outweigh her by at least a hundred pounds and stand my ground.

She looks up at me, sighs, then retrieves the envelope and leads me out of my grandmother's ballroom and to a nearby empty room.

"I don't want this to go *anywhere* but this room for today," she says, her voice strong, her tone saying it isn't open for discussion. "It's my best friend—my *cousin's* special day. Got it?"

I can't promise her that. But I nod. "I'll do everything I can not to ruin the day."

She blows out a breath and pulls a note out of the envelope, passing it to me.

If you do not meet our demands, we will send these to the press. Your family will be ruined. You will be ruined.

We will be in touch.

I scowl and look up at Annika. "Who the fuck sent this?"

"You know as much as I do." She shifts her feet.

"Show me the rest."

"No." She shakes her head quickly. "These are private photos, and I don't want you to see them. It's humiliating. You saw the last one."

What I thought I saw was Annika, naked, spread-eagle and tied to a bed with a group of men standing around her.

And by the look on her face, I'd say my memory isn't wrong.

I want to fucking *kill* someone.

I was her first. I knew everything about her, once upon a time.

Is this who she is now?

"I don't want to talk about it."

No. By the look on her face, I'd say that's not who she is. I have so many fucking questions.

"Here you are," Nadia says as she walks into the room, a bright smile on her face. "I thought I saw you leave. We're about to cut the cake."

The new bride stops talking and glances back and forth between us.

"What's wrong? Are you arguing again?"

"No." Annika pastes on a smile. "Of course, not. We were just talking."

"She needs to know."

The color leaves Annika's face, and Nadia turns to me, all badass now. "What the fuck is going on?"

Carmine walks in behind her and cocks a brow.

I pass them the note as Annika curses and paces away to look out the window.

"Who is this from?" Nadia asks, but Annika doesn't turn back from the window.

"We don't know," I reply softly. "There are photos, as well."

"Let me see," Nadia demands.

"No," Annika says, shaking her head. "Let's just forget this and go back to the party. We're ruining your day."

"Someone is *threatening* you," Carmine says, his voice much gentler than the look in his eyes. "Let us have the information, and if we can't handle it today, we'll tuck it away and push it aside until tomorrow."

Annika turns to him, her bottom lip trembling.

I want to pull her into my arms and assure her that everything will be okay.

But I can't.

She wouldn't welcome it, and I don't know that everything *will* be okay. I can't lie to her.

"Photos." She passes them to Nadia. "Do *not* show those to Carmine."

Nadia frowns, looks at the images, and then gasps. "*Annika.*"

"What are you guys doing in here?" Ivie asks as she and Shane walk in.

"Close and lock that door," I say to Shane, who frowns but does as I ask.

I quickly fill them in on what we know, which isn't much, and Nadia shows Ivie the photos.

"Jesus, Annika," Ivie breathes. "What in the ever-loving hell is this?"

Annika shakes her head, fights tears, and I go to her and take her hand, giving it a firm squeeze as I smile down at her.

"We're your friends and your family. You're safe here, honey."

She takes a deep breath.

"I really wish we didn't have to have this conversation right now—or ever." She licks her lips. "For now, let's just say that Richard was a son of a bitch. And after we got married, he turned into someone I didn't know. He had certain...*preferences.* If I denied him, he punished me, but also if I *agreed*—so to speak. Obviously, someone took photos, and they're trying to make a buck or two off of it. No biggie. I can afford to pay them to go away."

"Fuck that."

"No way."

"Absolutely, not."

Annika stares at all of us as we fume around her.

"You pay them this time, and they'll just come back for more," I inform her. "Besides, it doesn't say they want money. It doesn't specify the demands. I assume they'll be in touch again."

"I'll handle it." Her chin comes up, and she squares her shoulders. "I. Will. Handle. It. Now, I want all of you to go back to the party. Me, too, actually. I need a stiff drink."

"We're sticking close," I insist.

"Of course, you are. You're my people. Now, let's go have cake and champagne and get damn good and drunk in celebration."

We all exchange looks but nod and follow Annika back to the ballroom.

Carmine, Shane, and I hang back a bit as Ivie and Nadia flank Annika as they walk down the hall.

"We meet in the office at oh-nine-hundred," Carmine says. "All six of us. We'll figure this out."

"Copy that," I agree.

~

"OH, MY GOD, I'M HUNGOVER." Ivie walks into the office, makes a beeline for the coffee and donuts set up on the credenza, and sinks into a brown leather chair, her eyes closed. "Sugar will help."

"I feel great," Nadia says as she pours herself some coffee. "Must have been all that married sex we had all night long."

Carmine winks at his bride and takes a sip of his own coffee as Shane and Annika walk through the door.

"I found this one in the kitchen, sulking over a bowl of Cocoa Puffs."

She's still carrying the bowl.

"I'm not sulking."

"Well, you weren't smiling," Shane says and sits on the arm of Ivie's chair. "Hey, baby."

"Hey. I'm consuming all the sugar to help fight this hangover. I know better than to get drunk on champagne. It hurts."

"Drink lots of water today," Nadia advises her. "Okay, we're all here."

Carmine closes and locks the door. "I want to keep this between the six of us for a while. I don't think we need to involve the parents at this time."

"*You* don't have to be involved," Annika says. "Really, I can handle this."

"Can you?" Shane asks before I can. "Okay, what's your first move?"

"Nothing. I wait."

"Wrong," Shane replies. "We're going to question the staff. We're going to look at security disks. We're going to hunt these motherfuckers down and kill them."

"Can't I just sue them? Why do people have to die all the time?"

"Because they deserve it."

They deserve much more than just death.

And I'll be the one to hand it out.

"Nadia and Carmine are headed out on their honeymoon," Annika begins, but Nadia shakes her head.

"We're postponing, but only for a little while."

"No. No, Nadia. You deserve this break. Go on your honeymoon. I have these three looking out for me—whether I like it or not."

"Hey," Ivie says with a scowl, and I feel my lips twitch.

"Do you really think I'll just leave when this is going down?" Nadia demands. "Not a chance in hell. Besides, we'll get it wrapped up quickly, and I'll be lying on a tropical beach somewhere before I know it."

"I have a flight to catch this afternoon," Annika says, checking the time. "I'm headed back to Denver so I can get back to work."

"No."

She arches a brow at my one-word proclamation.

"Excuse me?"

"I didn't stutter. You're not taking a commercial flight."

She props her hands on her hips. "Yes, I am. I'm not like you. I don't always have to take a private jet."

"Someone is threatening you. That means you won't be on a commercial flight, Annika. When the time comes to go back to Denver, I'll fly you."

"The time is *today*," she stresses. "To. Day."

"God, you're stubborn." I push my hand through my hair and shake my head. "I'm not trying to control you or be an asshole here. I'm going to keep you safe, whether you like it or not."

"You're a caveman," she retorts.

Carmine smirks.

Shane coughs into his hand.

"Me, caveman." I thump my chest. "Me save you."

Annika just rolls her eyes.

"Ivie and I will get started on the security disks," Shane says and then smiles down at Ivie. "As soon as her head feels better."

"I need another donut." Before she can stand and retrieve it, Shane fetches it for her. "Thank you. I'll be good in a few minutes."

"I have a call in to the catering company to ask about the waiter who delivered the envelope," Carmine adds. "We'll get to the bottom of this."

"And what do I do in the meantime? Just sit around and wait?"

"You have your computer with you," Ivie points out.

"You can get caught up on charting, make calls to patients, that sort of thing."

Annika blows out a breath. "Fine. I'll be in my room, working."

She stomps away, and I want to run after her. My room is next to hers, and I heard her crying all night.

It's a personal torture, knowing that she hurts, but I know she wouldn't welcome my comfort.

"If I'm going to hack into stuff, I need more coffee," Ivie says.

"No one said you had to hack anything," Shane says with a laugh. "We *own* the security footage."

"Well, where's the fun in that?"

I blink at her, then look at Nadia. "What am I missing?"

"Ivie's killer with a computer," Shane says proudly. "She can hack into anything."

"Well, that'll come in handy." I grin and grab three donuts and a full cup of coffee, then head for the door. "I'll be in *my* room, making calls and keeping an eye on Annika. Just let me know if you find anything. I'll do the same."

The others nod as I stride out of the office and head up the stairs to the bedrooms.

I know my grandmother's old home like the back of my hand. My brothers and I practically grew up here. Since she died, it feels like we've spent even more time here.

That would make Gram happy.

I stop by Annika's door and press my ear against the wood.

The water's running.

She's in the shower.

I walk into my space and shove a donut into my mouth while I boot up my computer.

CHAPTER 2

~ANNIKA~

*N*o matter how much I try or how long I stand under the hot water, it won't wash away the filth I've seen or done. It won't make me feel clean.

I turn off the taps and reach for a towel, wrap my hair, and then grab another for my body.

I'm actually relieved that I don't have to go sit on a plane today. I don't have to keep my shit together. I can hide away in this pretty room.

Once I'm dry, I pull a fluffy robe around me and get into bed, pulling the covers over my head.

And feel the tears come.

I thought that with Richard gone, I'd be able to forget about all of the horrible things he did and made *me* do and move on with my life.

But he just keeps hurting me, even from the grave.

"A?"

I sigh at Nadia's knock, then fling the covers back and walk to the door. I unlock it and crack it open.

"Yeah?"

"Can I come in? I brought provisions."

"I'm coming!" Ivie hurries down the hallway, out of breath. "I have the coffee."

"Come on in." I turn away and lie on the bed once more, but don't cover my face with the blankets. "I'm not really in the mood for a party, though. And I feel *awful* about this, Nadia. You're supposed to be off on your honeymoon, having wild sex and relaxing. I didn't mean to fuck that up for you."

"I already told you," Nadia replies as she passes me a maple bar, "I'm still going, just a few days later than planned. This isn't your fault."

"Yes." I take a bite, but it just feels like cardboard in my mouth. "It is my fault."

"I personally think it's a waste of time to argue about fault," Ivie says and sits on the bench at the end of the bed, facing me. "I'm quite sure you didn't hire someone to blackmail you at Nadia's wedding."

I take another bite. "No. That would be dumb."

"Exactly." Nadia grins at me, but her blue eyes are full of worry. "Honey, let's not talk about the blackmail part because that's being handled. What I want to know is, what's in those photos? Tell me they're photoshopped and it's not you."

It would be so easy to deny it. To take that line and insist that it isn't me in the pictures.

But I don't like to lie. And I'm not good at it.

"I didn't find out until after we got married that Rich was into some really weird stuff. At least, weird to me. There are people in the lifestyle, consensually, who enjoy it. But, I'm not one of them."

"Are you telling me he *made* you do that? That's rape, Annika." Ivie scowls.

"I guess I had a choice. I could either agree to it, or he would punish me for days if I said no. Sometimes, the punishment was worse than just going along with him. I had no idea that I was being recorded."

I pace over to the windows and look out across the green, manicured grounds of the estate. The cleanup crew is here, disassembling the gorgeous wedding that took several months to plan.

"Someday, we're going to unpack all of this baggage that Dick brought into your life," Nadia says. "And the carry-on luggage that I carry because Alex had a hand in it."

"We all need therapy," Ivie adds and takes a sip of her coffee. "We're some fucked-up people."

"I think we're pretty great," I say, watching my best friends fuss over me. "We may be fucked-up in some ways, but we're awesome in plenty of others."

"Hell yes, we are," Nadia agrees. "Do you think it's smart to go back to Denver right now? We could all stay here for a little longer. It's safer. I don't like the thought of you being in that big house alone when these assholes are out there carrying a grudge."

"I'm selling the house," I announce. "It goes on the market next week. I don't want to live there. Too many memories."

I won't even get into the fact that one of the photos in that awful envelope was taken in my basement.

"I think that's a good idea," Ivie says. "It's a lot of house for one person anyway."

"I think I want a condo. Downtown. Something close to restaurants and shopping."

"Sounds perfect to me," Nadia says. "You know I love house hunting, so if you want help looking, I'm your girl."

"Count me in," Ivie agrees. "Okay, I have to go work my computer skills for my fiancé. He thinks I'm hot when I'm typing away at a keyboard. Maybe I'll wear something sexy, just to make things fun."

I laugh and reach for another donut. "Keep us posted. And maybe call a doctor because I'm pretty sure we're about to put ourselves into sugar shock with all of these donuts."

"We'll have a salad for lunch." Ivie winks and leaves the room, closing the door behind her.

"Nadia," I say when we're alone. "Are you sure I can't talk you into going on your honeymoon today as planned?"

"You're stuck with me," she says. "Someone is trying to hurt someone I love, A. What would you do?"

"The same thing," I admit. "I'd do the same damn thing."

"Exactly. So, stop worrying about me. We'll get it all figured out, bust some kneecaps, send someone swimming with the fishes, and be on our way."

I can't help the snort of laughter that escapes at that descriptive image. "You're such a mobster."

"Thanks." Nadia winks. "I have to warn you. If we can't resolve this soon, we're going to have to bring in my father."

I shake my head, but Nadia keeps talking.

"He'll be beyond pissed if we keep something big like this from him. I wanted to warn you because he'll want to see the photos."

"Jesus, Nadia, I don't want him to see that. I don't want *anyone* to see it." The tears start again. "It's so humiliating. Please, don't tell him."

"I won't. Yet. We might have this all resolved by tomorrow morning."

"I hope so."

Nadia pulls me in for a tight hug. "You're an amazing woman, A. You've been through hell and back, and yet you're thriving. I'm proud of you."

"Stop making me cry."

She laughs and kisses my cheek before pulling away. "Okay, no more being mushy. Take the day to rest. Nap. Work. Whatever. I'll keep you posted."

"Thanks."

〜

"YOU HAVE to get out of this bed."

I shift under the covers and crack an eye to find Ivie frowning down at me.

"Why?"

"Because it's been two days, and you've barely moved."

I know I'm being a coward. Weak. I should be facing this head-on, the way Ivie or Nadia would. But, damn it, I'm just so *tired.*

"Sleepy."

"Honey, you're starting to smell bad."

I crack that eye again and scowl at my best friend. "Thanks."

"Come on. Up. In the shower. I have dinner here for you, but you can't have it until you scrub up. And for the love of all that's holy, brush your teeth."

"You're really good for my ego, you know that? So much for being my best friend. I might replace you."

"Uh-huh. Right. Get in there."

She pulls me to my feet and pushes me toward the bathroom. "I'm going. God, you're bossy."

"You haven't seen anything yet, sister."

"Being in love has made you sassy, and I don't know if I like it."

"You love me. Now, go."

She closes the door behind me, and I take a second to stare at my reflection in the mirror.

She's right. This is ridiculous. And I look like hell.

So, I take my time in the shower, shave all the places I've neglected, and then brush my teeth.

When I open the bathroom door, she's set up a tray by the window, complete with a red rose in a bud vase.

"Are we on a date?" I ask her.

"Eating on a pretty table will make you feel better. It's a chicken Caeser salad with lemon on the side and a chocolate torte for dessert."

"My favorite." I sink into the chair, and my stomach growls loudly. "I'm hungry."

"I bet you are. You've hardly eaten anything since the donuts yesterday."

I take a big bite of salad and frown at Ivie. "Are you keeping track?"

"Hell, yes, I am. Someone has to. After dinner, we're having a meeting with the others."

That means I'll have to see Rafe.

And that makes me nervous under the best of circumstances. With things the way they currently are, it almost makes me lose my appetite.

"Eat."

"You know, the whole hovering and shoving food into my mouth thing isn't a good look for you."

"That's okay," she says smoothly. "You look better."

The salad is delicious. I can't stop shoveling it in.

"I'm feeling better." When the plate is empty, I shift to the chocolate and sigh in delight after the first bite. "Oh, God."

"I know, right? So good."

"You ate it, too?"

"Yes, we already had dinner. We invited you, but you didn't answer."

I sigh and lick the spoon. "I slept a lot. Sleep has always been my escape from bad things."

"I know."

"And it's time to wake up and face this." I sit back and sigh, contentedly full. "Okay, lead the way to the meeting."

Ivie raises a brow. "Are you going to wear that?"

I look down at the towel wrapped around me and laugh. "Uh, no. I guess I'd better put something on."

I grab leggings and a teal blue sweatshirt and throw my wet hair up in a messy bun. I'm no fashionista, but it's an improvement.

"Better?"

"Much. Okay, let's go."

We walk downstairs together. Everyone else is already waiting in the family room off the kitchen, dressed in casual clothes and laughing at something Carmine said.

"There she is," Nadia says with a smile. "How are you doing, sugar?"

"Better. I'm done sleeping, I think. Now it's time to kick ass."

"Good girl," Rafe murmurs as he sidles up next to me and takes my hand.

I want to pull it away.

Not because I don't want him touching me. Exactly

the opposite. It feels too damn good, and I don't want to get into the habit of feeling him close.

But I'm too weak to pull back right now.

So, I give his hand a squeeze and smile at the others.

"Okay, friends, what do we know?"

"The kid who brought you the envelope was hired by the catering company to be a server. We talked to him, and he said that someone passed it to him. He can't remember who because it was busy at that time." Shane leans forward and takes Ivie's hand. "We do have footage of a car coming and going, but when Ivie ran the plates, she found it's a rental."

"So, I did some hacking," Ivie picks up. "Of course, the name of the person who rented it is John Doe."

"Seriously?" I take my hand from Rafe's, immediately feeling the loss, and prop my hands on my hips. "The rental company allowed someone named *John Doe* to take their car?"

"They probably did everything online," Rafe points out. "Didn't even have to see a live person to pick it up."

"Technology doesn't always help," I mutter. "Were you able to figure out who John Doe is?"

"No." Ivie bites her lip. "Sorry, it was a dead end."

"So, we're back to square one."

"Not square one," Carmine says. "We're aware of what's happening, and we can be on the offensive. They're going to try to reach out to you again. It's just a matter of when and where."

"I'm not going to simply sit here and wait." Rafe

starts to interrupt, but I shake my head. "This is ridiculous. Maybe they just wanted to scare me. Who knows? I have a life to get back to. Patients. A clinic to run. So, I'm going back to my life, and all of you should, too. While keeping an ear to the ground, of course."

"She's right," Shane says before anyone can object, surprising everyone in the room, including me. "We don't know when or if they'll contact her again. I believe they will. I think it'll be sooner than later, but not as long as she's in this fortress, and we're all on the lookout."

"See? I'm right."

"She should go back to Denver. Back to her life. We'll go with her and strategically protect her."

"Wait. That's not what I meant."

Shane shakes his head. "You need to get back to *normal*, so to speak, to make them think that you're not worried about what they'll do. But you know as well as everyone else in this room that we won't just drop you off and wish you well, Annika."

"Hell, no," Rafe agrees. "We all go."

"This is really annoying." I rub my forehead in frustration. "The most annoying part is that you're probably right."

And I don't want to admit that it makes me feel better, safer, to know that they'll all be close by. The thought of going back on my own is terrifying.

"Can we go tomorrow?" I ask.

"The plane will be ready anytime you are," Rafe assures me.

"Looks like we're going to Denver," Nadia says. "I like it there."

"Ivie and I are going to the ranch for a couple of days to check in with Curt and make sure everything is good there," Shane says. "But we can be back in Denver within an hour if something goes wrong."

"I'll be back at work with you by Monday," Ivie assures me. "Thanks for all the time off."

"You've more than earned it." It's the absolute truth. Ivie hasn't taken a vacation from being my office manager since we opened the Medi-spa's doors two years ago. "I'll check in with Deidre when we get there to make sure the office is ready to reopen next week."

"I already did," Ivie says. "She assured me that everything is good to go."

I nod and suddenly feel eighty years old. The past year has aged me. I'm exhausted.

But I'm not going to lose this fight. Someone is dicking with me, and I'm so over being the pawn in other people's games.

We're going to finish this.

And then I'm going to start rebuilding my life and live it exactly as I want.

With no excuses or apologies.

CHAPTER 3

"Okay, so Nadia and Carmine are just a mile away," I say as I help Annika into her house with her bags. It's late in the evening. Annika wanted to come earlier in the day, but Carmine had some things to see to, and one thing led to another, so we didn't leave the city until well after dinner.

But we made it.

I follow her to her bedroom and set the suitcases on the bed so she can easily unpack them. "You're not in the master?"

"Hell, no." Her grin doesn't reach her eyes. "I'll never set foot in that room again. I'd rather not be *here*, but it's not for much longer."

She doesn't meet my gaze as she unzips one bag and starts emptying dirty laundry into a basket.

"How can I help?" Jesus, I want to touch her. I want to pull her to me and kiss the fuck out of her like I used to. It used to be that I didn't have to ask to be near her. We were like magnets; we couldn't keep our hands off of each other.

I used to know every little detail about her.

And now, she might as well be a stranger.

It makes me fucking crazy.

"Rafe, you've gone above and beyond," she says with a small sigh. "I'll set the alarm after you leave. Everything should be just fine here."

I scowl and can't hold back from reaching for her. I take her hand in mine, and she looks up in surprise.

"I'm not leaving."

"Of course, you're leaving."

"Annika, I'm here to protect you. I can't do that from some hotel room."

"Listen, Rafe, I appreciate that you want to help, but—"

"Is that what you think this is? That I'm just here to *help* like I'm some fucking Boy Scout, A?"

"You're my friend."

I push a hand through my hair and have to clench my jaw so I don't yell that I'm here because I'm in love with her.

I've been in love with her for almost a decade, goddamn it.

"Yeah. I'm your friend." I can't help that the word *friend* sounds like a dirty word. "I'm not leaving."

"Well, you know what they say? You don't have to go home, but you can't stay here."

I narrow my eyes at her, and she just cocks a hip and sets her hand on it, nothing but stubbornness and sass.

God, I want to kiss her so badly, I ache with it.

But now is not the time. I don't know when it'll *be* the time.

"Fine."

I turn and walk out of the room, down the stairs, and out the front door. I don't stop until I get to my rental car, slamming the door behind me before settling in for a long damn night in the cramped space.

Because I'm not leaving, no matter what she fucking says.

What I said the other day is completely true. I want to eat her with a damn spoon and spank her, all at the same time. She's infuriating. She always was, but now that I can't touch her, *be* with her, it's even more so.

Damn woman.

I've just reclined the seat and found an easy-listening station on the radio when Annika opens her front door, frowns and me, and comes stomping to the car.

I roll down the window.

"Problem?" I ask.

"What are you doing?"

"Listening to the radio. Keeping an eye out. You know, the usual."

She shakes her head and blinks furiously, the way she does when she's frustrated.

"Why are you out here in the car like a stalker?"

"Not a stalker. I'm on a stakeout. Since you won't let me stay in *there*,"—I gesture to the house—"I'm going to be out here instead. It's not the best of circumstances, but I have heat, and I can always order a pizza or something."

"You'll order a pizza." She laughs and shakes her head. "And what? Tell them to deliver it to the car in my driveway?"

"Sure. Is that weird?"

"Yeah, Rafe, it's weird. Just go to the hotel. I'll talk to you tomorrow."

"Like you said, I don't have to go home, but I can't stay here. Well, I'm not in there. And if you don't want me in your driveway, I can park at the curb."

She watches me for several seconds—to see if I'm bluffing, I'm sure.

I'm not.

"Fine. Have it your way. Stay in the car in the driveway, Rafe. You'll last one night, and then you'll be at the hotel tomorrow night."

"Don't bet on it, sweetheart."

"Why are you so stubborn?"

"Hi, pot, I'm kettle."

She growls in frustration and marches back to the house, glaring at me over her shoulder before slamming the door shut.

I hoped she'd cave and let me back inside. Hell, I'd settle for the couch at this point.

But that's not my Annika. No, the woman has more backbone, more stubbornness in her little finger than most people have in their whole bodies.

It's one of the reasons why I love her to distraction.

A pizza doesn't sound half bad, so I make a call and entertain myself as I wait by checking in with my contacts to see if there's been any additional chatter about the current situation with Annika.

There hasn't been.

The pizza kid parks behind me, and I get out to intercept the pizza.

"Uh, hi," he says and swallows hard. "That's thirty-seven-fifty."

I pass him a fifty. "Keep the change."

"Solid. Thanks." He flashes a smile. "Are you surprising someone with pizza or something?"

"Something like that," I agree and nod when he turns to leave. Once he's gone, I take one of the two boxes, set it on the porch in front of the door, and then return to my car and open my box.

I type out a quick text to Annika.

Me: *Dinner's on the porch. Better fetch it before it goes cold.*

There's no reply, but then, I don't expect one. I'm halfway into my second slice when the door opens, and Annika stares down at the pizza box. She glances up at me, picks up the box, and takes it inside.

Pepperoni with olives is her favorite. She'll be out in no time, telling me to come inside and eat with her.

There's no way she'll leave me out here all night. She may be stubborn, but she has a soft side.

And I can usually get there through her stomach.

But I finish off all but two pieces of my pie, and still no Annika.

Two hours later, when there's nothing left for me to do but sit and watch the neighborhood, she *still* hasn't said a word.

"She's seriously going to leave me out here." I shake my head and can't help but laugh. "Is it any wonder I want to spend the rest of my life with her?"

BAM! Bam! Bam!

I startle and open my eyes. Shit, I fell asleep.

"Good morning," I mutter as I roll down the window. "What time is it?"

"Six," she replies, but her mouth softens into a smile. "You really stayed out here."

"Of course." I wipe my mouth, conscious of the stubble on my face. "Last time I looked at the time, it was four-thirty. So, I wasn't out long."

"Come on, tough guy. I'll make you some coffee."

"And pancakes?"

She shakes her head, but she's laughing. "Sure, I'll make pancakes. I also have leftover pizza."

"Me, too." I grab a few things from the car. When

we turn to walk back into the house, I scowl. "What the fuck is that?"

"What?" She looks up and then gasps. "Oh, God. I didn't see it when I came outside. But I was looking at you."

"Motherfucker," I growl and stomp up the steps but don't take the envelope off the door yet. I take my phone from my pocket and call Carmine. "We have another envelope. Haven't opened it yet."

"Jesus, it's six in the goddamn morning. Give us thirty and we'll be there."

He ends the call.

"I need gloves."

"Be right back," Annika says and slips through the door, avoiding the envelope like it's a snake that might strike out and bite her, then hurries back to me with a gardening glove.

"You don't have any latex gloves?" I ask, scowling at the glove in my hand.

"No, I'm out."

"This won't fit me."

"Oh. Right. You have big hands. I can get a baggie or something."

I pass the glove back to her. "It's okay. You put it on and grab the envelope."

"No."

She firms her lips and shakes her head.

"It can't hurt you."

41

She stares at me for a long moment. "I'm quite sure that whatever's in there will hurt me."

I blow out a breath and use the glove to take the envelope off the door, careful not to add prints to it. We'll have Shane run it later, along with whatever's inside.

He ran the last ones, but the evidence was contaminated with too many other fingerprints to find anything useful.

We move inside, close the door, and I lay the letter on the dining room table. I text Carmine and ask him to bring gloves.

"I can't believe I didn't see that when I opened the door," Annika mutters. She walks into the kitchen and gets to work making coffee. "I guess I was too focused on you."

The last words are a whisper, but I heard them.

"A—"

"I always was," she continues as if she has to fill the silence with words. "I couldn't see anything *but* you for years. Is it weird that it was the best time of my life?"

"No." I swallow and fist my hands because they itch to hold her. "It's not weird."

"It's silly," she says and then blushes a bit. "I shouldn't have said that."

"Hey, we're friends. We used to be much more than that. And you can trust me. You can say *anything* to me."

"No." She turns to me, her big, blue eyes full of tears. "I can't. I can't, Rafe."

"Sweetheart—"

"Hello?" Nadia calls out from the front door. "Where are you guys?"

"Kitchen," Annika calls back but hasn't taken her gaze away from mine. "Let's just deal with this, okay?"

"Yeah. Okay."

"I'm making coffee," Annika announces to Nadia and Carmine. "There's cream and sugar and anything else you could want around the kitchen here."

"Excellent," Nadia says as she leads Carmine into the room. Her short hair is still a little disheveled, and her face is clean of makeup, her eyes sleepy. "We came right over, but I did insist that we make a quick stop at the donut place down the street."

"God bless you," I reply and reach into the pink box for a cinnamon twist. "I think, given the turn of events, my homemade pancakes are off the table for today."

"You'll live," Annika says and sets a mug of steaming coffee in front of me.

"When and where was the package left?" Nadia asks.

"It was taped to the front door." I sigh in frustration. "I fell asleep for ninety fucking minutes, and they slipped past me. Jesus."

"Not your fault," Carmine says. "And, this is a new clue."

"I have cameras," Annika announces, surprising me.

43

"What?"

"I had them installed after Ivie was taken," she explains as if she's discussing new gutters or rosebushes. "There's probably something on them."

"I know we're all sleepy," Nadia says as she chomps on a maple bar, "but you should have started with that information."

"I'm tired, and I'm frustrated, and it just occurred to me." Annika shrugs and drinks her black coffee. "Should we call Shane and Ivie?"

"Already did," Carmine says. "They'll be here in about an hour. Less now."

"We'll wait, then," Annika says. "I'm not exactly in a hurry to open that envelope, and I assume Shane will want to look for fingerprints."

"That's ideal," I reply, watching her. She's fidgety. Nervous. "Honey, what are you afraid of finding in there?"

"What? Oh, I couldn't tell you."

What in the bloody hell did that piece of shit make her do? I want to ask. I want her to feel comfortable enough with me to tell me everything so I can help her. So I can make the bad memories go away and replace them with new, happy ones.

But she won't open up to me.

And it's making me damn crazy.

We've made our way through a second round of coffee when Ivie throws open the door and comes running inside, straight for Annika.

"Are you okay? What did they leave? Oh, God, I'm so sorry that I was so far away."

"Hey, it's okay." Annika hugs Ivie and pats her back in reassurance. "I'm fine. It's been really boring, actually."

"We didn't open it yet," I inform Shane. "Thought you'd like to check it out first."

"Thanks," he says with a nod and points to the envelope at the other end of the table. "That it?"

"Yeah."

My brother sets a case on the table next to it and starts fiddling with dust and brushes.

"No prints," he announces.

"Well, damn." I sigh and drain my mug, then look at Annika. "Looks like you're up, honey."

She wrinkles her nose. "I was hoping to stall a little longer."

"Let's get it over with. Then we'll know what we're dealing with," Nadia suggests. "Ivie and I are right here. We're *all* here. You're safe."

Annika nods and walks to the end of the table. She takes the envelope from Shane and breaks the seal.

"I used to love getting mail," she says conversationally. "I would wait every day for the mail carrier and hope there would be something for me. Anything at all. Even junk mail. I know it's silly, but I always looked forward to it.

"And then this happens. Now, I'll never want to check my mailbox again."

"Open it," I say, my voice calm and soft. "Let's see what we've got, then we'll look at the security video."

She nods and pulls a stack of sheets out of the large envelope. We all sit facing her so we can't see what she's looking at.

Her blue eyes shift from guarded curiosity to embarrassment to confusion. And then, just when I'm about to rush to her and take everything out of her hands so I can see, those eyes turn fierce and angry.

And I know, without a shadow of a doubt, that the game has changed for her.

She's pissed.

CHAPTER 4

~ANNIKA~

*W*ith all five of them staring at me, I rip open the envelope and pull out the contents. Just like last time, there's a note on top.

Now that we have your attention, let's talk terms. We don't want money. That's too...cliché. No, Annika, we want you. Based on what we've seen you do and know you're capable of, what your tastes are, this shouldn't be a problem.

We'll be in touch very soon.

Jesus. I swallow hard and steel myself to flip to the photos.

The first is like the others. I'm tied up on a bed covered with satin sheets. I'm naked. No one else is in the photo.

I flip to another and have to bite the inside of my cheek so I don't gasp in terror. My God, how is it possible that someone took *photos* of this? Of what those men did to me?

I hurry to the next.

There's a yellow sticky note on the last one.

In case you plan to deny us, perhaps you should consider that we know what you did. What you were involved in. Drug distribution is a federal crime.

It's a photo of me walking out of my clinic with my briefcase, simply leaving work.

But they're implying that I knew that Richard was a drug dealer, and they're threatening to call the cops.

Fuck. That.

"What is it?" Nadia asks.

"More of the same." I sigh and stuff it all back into the envelope. "But they're more specific about what they want now."

"How much?" Carmine asks. My gaze meets his, and I shake my head.

"They don't want money."

"What in the hell *do* they want?" Rafe demands.

"Me." I toss the envelope onto the table and try to control the shaking in my hands. "Also, they're implying that I knew about Rich's drug distribution, and state that if I don't give them what they want, they'll turn me in."

"Blackmail *and* extorsion," Ivie says. "They're a bunch of overachievers."

I grin at her. It's either that or throw something. "Clearly, they won't get *me*."

"What, exactly," Rafe says, rage coming from him in waves, "do you mean by they want *you*?"

I lick my lips. "Sexually."

"Motherfucker son of a bitch," he growls and starts prowling my dining room. "I'm going to fucking kill them. Every one of them. Slowly."

"Let's look at your security footage," Shane suggests.

"Good idea." I walk past Rafe but stop to lay my hand on his shoulder. "It's going to be okay, you know."

"As soon as I kill the son of a bitch who's doing *that*," —he points to the table—"yeah, it'll be fine."

I pat his shoulder, try not to acknowledge the bulging muscles under his shirt, and go to fetch my laptop.

Ivie holds her hand up for it and grins at Shane.

"I got this, babe." She opens the computer, taps the keyboard, finds my software, and narrows her eyes. "Okay, so this would have been dropped off between four-thirty and six. Let's see what we've got."

She blows out a raspberry. Shane looks over her shoulder. The rest of us just stare at her, waiting with bated breath.

"Got him." She taps a key, and we all crowd in behind Ivie to see what she found. "Look, right here at five-fifteen."

"He's in a hoodie and a mask," Nadia says.

"And stays close to the wall," Carmine adds. "We can't see enough of him to figure out who the fuck he is."

"I agree," Ivie says with a nod. "But he messed up.

He runs back to his car and drives in front of the house. I can blow this up and pull the plate."

"What if it's John Doe again?" I ask.

"I have a good feeling about this one. Give me a little room and a smidge of time."

"That's code for stop crowding her," I say as we back away. "I need more coffee."

"I'll take another donut," Nadia adds and joins me in the kitchen. "Talk to me. We're alone."

"What do you want me to say?"

"Tell me how you feel, sugar." She takes my shoulders in her hands and gives me *the look*. The one she always uses when she thinks I'm not telling her everything.

"I'm pissed." I sigh and push my hand through my hair. "I'm just so *mad*, Nadia. Who the fuck is doing this, and who do they think they are, thinking they can treat me like this? I didn't do anything to anyone. I just want to live my boring life in suburbia. Mind my own business. But that just can't seem to happen, and it's driving me *crazy*."

"Well, I'm glad you're past feeling sorry for yourself and landed squarely in being angry. It's a nice change."

I narrow my eyes at her, but she just grins.

"Okay, I've got something," Ivie calls out. "The plates aren't linked to a John Doe but rather a Larry MacDonald. We have a place to start digging."

"Thank God. What do we do now?"

"We're going to the office," Shane says. "We have

better equipment there. I'll do a deep-dive on this MacDonald asshole. If we're lucky, we can pay him a visit later today."

"I'll come with you," I reply.

"No." Rafe shakes his head. "We don't know who we're dealing with, and you haven't trained for this, A."

"So I just sit here and let you all do my dirty work?"

"Yes." Nadia kisses my cheek. "You're too pretty to kill people, A."

I roll my eyes and watch as they all gather their things and go, leaving Rafe and I behind.

"Aren't you going with them?"

"No." He shifts his feet. "I'm staying here with you."

"I don't need a babysitter, Rafe."

"Didn't say you did. But you need a friend."

I sigh. "Is that what you are? My friend?"

"Absolutely." He smiles that charming smile I can never say no to.

"Fine, you can stay. I have some work to do, so I'll be in my office if you need me."

"Where can I set up shop?" he asks. "Here in the dining room?"

"It's not very comfortable." I frown, taking in the formal table and stiff, high-backed chairs. "There's a desk in the guest room. It'll be more comfortable. Come on, I'll show you."

He lifts his bag off the floor and follows me up the stairs. I can feel his eyes on my ass. He always did have a thing for my behind.

"It's just a butt, Rafe."

"A grade-A one," he agrees, his voice filled with a grin.

God, I missed flirting with him.

The guest room is on the second door on the left. I open it and usher him inside.

"You can use anything you need. But really, Rafe, wouldn't you be more comfortable at the hotel?"

"Are you kidding me? You think a hotel is better than this? No." He grins and sets his bag on the bed. "Thanks for the loan. Do you mind if I borrow the shower in this attached bathroom?"

Rafe is going to be naked. In my house.

Lord have mercy.

"Of course, not."

His blue eyes sparkle as he winks at me. "Thanks."

"Okay. I have some charting to catch up on, and I need to review cases for next week. If you need anything, I'm just downstairs. Oh, and you can't stay here tonight."

"Annika."

"Nope. No way." I shake my head and turn to leave the room.

Rafe Martinelli will *not* be sleeping under my roof. No way, no how.

HE'S in his car again.

I pace my bedroom, sipping wine. He's just so damn stubborn, that's what it is. He thinks he has to *protect* me. But Shane and Ivie are *this* close to figuring out where all of this is coming from, and then it'll be over. Probably by tomorrow.

He doesn't have to stay.

Okay, so it feels kind of good knowing that he's right there, in the *very* slim chance that something was to happen.

"You can't let him sleep outside again." I walk through the house, set the wine on the table by the front door, tighten the belt on my robe, and walk outside.

Rafe watches as I approach his car. He rolls down the window.

"Problem?" he asks.

"Yes. You're in my driveway. I know, I can't talk you into going to the hotel. Come on. You can crash in the guest room."

"I'm fine out here, if you'd rather."

"Clearly, I don't rather." I open the door and wait while he closes everything down and snags his bag. "I can't leave you out here for another night. No matter how crazy you make me, I feel bad."

"I make you crazy?" He flashes a smile, and I have to turn away and walk to the house before I do something stupid like kiss him silly. "Tell me more about that."

"No." I hold the door for him and then close and lock it. "Want some wine?"

"Nah, I'm good."

I nod and walk into the kitchen to refill my glass, then gesture for Rafe to join me in the family room. This is one of my favorite spaces. It's cozy with deep-cushioned couches, colorful pillows and throws, and a TV.

I sit, toss a blanket over my lap, and sip while Rafe kicks off his shoes and curls up in the couch across from me.

I'm already feeling the effects of the wine. Just a little. And that's good because I could use a little buzz tonight.

It's been a hell of a week.

"So, what's new?" I ask and get the laugh I expected. His laugh always made my stomach clench.

Nothing has changed in that department. God, he's a sight to behold. "What is it about men getting better-looking as they age?"

He tilts his head. "Did you just call me old?"

I snort and take another sip. "No. I said you're getting better-looking as you get older. There's a difference."

"I miss you," he says and rubs his hand over his face. "Do you know how hard it is to sit over here, see that you're struggling, and not hold you?"

I don't know what to say to that, so I sip my wine. The small buzz has progressed into a pleasant, bigger buzz now.

"You're a good person," I reply.

"Fuck that." He shakes his head and braces his elbows on his knees, leaning forward. "I'm not a good person, A. I've done some shitty things in this life."

"Me, too." I stare down into my glass and think about what he said earlier about being my friend. Maybe I need to talk about this. And it's not like I can be with him for the long haul, so who better to talk to? "The pictures they sent... The things that Richard made me do. It was pretty bad."

I take another drink for courage and watch as Rafe sits back again, his eyes pinned to mine, listening.

"We dated for *years* before we got married. I thought I knew him inside and out. He was smart and funny and gentle. Kind of boring, truth be told, but I was okay with boring. You know that."

He just watches, so I keep talking.

"Then we got married, and it all changed. Not overnight, either. It changed that *day*. Suddenly, the man I thought I knew was gone, replaced by this cold, mean man that I didn't recognize at all. He liked to punish me. Got off on it, I think. And he liked some weird sexual shit, Rafe. He liked to watch. And other... things. If I said no, he got angry. Furious. It wasn't just the run-of-the-mill silent treatment or yelling and then getting over it.

"No, he'd rant and rave. Lecture. Take my car away. One night, he locked me out of the house."

"He locked you out of your own house?"

"It wasn't mine. My name wasn't on it. It's only

mine now because he died and left it to me. He was a horrible person. So, I learned that it was just easier to go along with what he wanted. At first, he only wanted other people to watch. That was awful. But then, it just...got worse. I'm not going to go into the details because they're embarrassing and awful. But I did those things, Rafe. Even if it made me sick. Even if I didn't want to. I still did them."

"You were terrorized," he says, his blue eyes shooting flames of anger. "Enslaved. Abused doesn't even start to cover it. Christ, A, if I'd known—"

"It's over now." I shift in my seat and frown at my empty glass. "My lips are numb. I should probably stop drinking now."

"You should go to bed."

"Yeah." I blink at him. "You're so handsome. And I'm still just as drawn to you as I was when I was nineteen. Too bad it didn't work out. Well, I'm going to bed. Make yourself at home."

I wave and wander up the stairs to my room, take the robe off, and climb into bed.

I'm just *so tired.*

But then the dreams come.

"You're going to lie on that bed and let me do whatever I want to you, Annika."

I scowl and try to keep the tears at bay. "Richard, this makes me uncomfortable."

"I don't fucking care. You're mine. That means you'll do

what I say, when I say. Now, get on the bed with your ass in the air like I told you to."

I let the tears fall, but I know they won't matter. Richard never cares what I say or do, as long as he can use me the way he wants. He's awful. He's evil.

People are watching, but I close my eyes and block it out. I'm at the beach, in a chair, with the sun shining on my face.

For just a moment, I almost believe it.

But then something hits me over the butt, hard. *I cry out, but it keeps happening, over and over, making my skin sting and more tears come to my eyes.*

God, is it over yet?

But, no. No, it's not.

They take turns. Some fuck me. Others laugh. Touch. I'm nothing but a thing to them. I'm nothing.

"He'll never want you now," Richard hisses in my ear. "You're damaged goods, and Rafe will never look at you with anything but disgust. You're a slut. A whore."

"No." I clench my fists and cry out again. *"No, please. Just stop. I'll be good. Just stop."*

"Hey, baby. Hey. You're okay."

He pulls me to him, and I want to cling to him. To tell Rafe how much I love him. To thank him for making me feel safe.

But the words won't come, and the dreams won't stop.

CHAPTER 5

~RAFE~

*T*he screaming woke me. The whimpers tore at my heart. No man wants to hear the love of his life cry out in terror.

And now, holding her hand in the dark, I'm torn between needing to comfort her and wanting to kill someone.

I've never felt the need to murder the way I do on Annika's behalf. I'm the least violent of the three of us brothers. But she's hurting, and someone needs to pay.

The worst part is, I have a feeling that the person responsible for the anguish is already dead.

I should go back to my own bed now that she seems to be settled down, but she's so damn tempting.

Just leave her be, Martinelli.

I turn to leave, but she whimpers again, and I make the executive decision to stay. I slip between the covers and spoon her, pulling her against me as a million memories flood my mind.

I spent *years* sleeping with her just like this. Years. It's as familiar as breathing. Sometimes, we wouldn't sleep at all. We'd lie in the dark and talk and laugh. Other times, we'd make love all night long.

I miss all of it. Every minute of it. The fact that I can't be with her because of who our families are makes me rage like nothing else ever has.

"Damaged goods," she says, talking in her sleep.

"Shh." I smooth her hair away from her face and kiss her cheek. "It's okay."

"Rafe won't want me."

I blink, surprised. What the hell kind of dream is this? In what alternate universe would I ever *not* want her?

"Not good enough."

"Hey, babe. Hey." I kiss her again and brush my fingers down her cheek. She wiggles onto her back, her eyes flutter open, and she offers me a half-smile. "You're safe, Annika."

"Safe." She sighs, burrows into my shoulder, and seems to calm down.

Does she think she's not good enough for me? That *anything* she may have done in her past would make me want her any less? That I could ever fall out of love with her? For Christ's sake, I've loved her all of my adult life.

If that's the case, we need to have a serious conversation because it couldn't be further from the truth.

I've tried to tell her for years that I want her. Even when she was married to that no-good piece of trash. And I'm not proud of that. Being married is a commitment that I believe in. I don't poach on someone else's territory.

But she doesn't belong to him anymore. She never really did, given she didn't know who she was marrying.

She's *mine.*

And I'm going to do everything I can to remind her of that.

"Don't go," she whispers.

"Wild horses couldn't drag me away, sweetheart."

She falls back to sleep, more peacefully now, and I kiss her forehead and then let sleep settle around me, too. I'm exhausted.

It feels like I just closed my eyes when the house alarms start blaring shrilly through the house.

"Rafe!" Annika yells, already leaping from the bed. "Rafe!"

"I'm right here," I reply as I climb out of the other side of the bed.

She whirls around and frowns. "What are you doing *in my bed?*"

"Seriously?" I shake my head. The alarm continues going crazy. "Now isn't the time for this conversation. Do you have a weapon?"

"I have a baseball bat."

I swear under my breath. "We have some work to do. Stay here. Lock the door. I'm going to take care of this."

"Be careful," she hisses before I shut the door behind me. I don't have shoes or a shirt. No weapon on me.

Because I'm an idiot.

Or a man in love, and Annika needed me.

Either way, it's no excuse.

I rush down the hall to the guest room, and when I see that no one's in there, I grab my pistol and shove my feet into my shoes.

Then, I make my way downstairs.

If it's a random robbery, they should have been scared off by the alarm and long gone by now. If it's a mistake in the system, we can fix that.

But if it's tied to the other shit happening, someone might be inside the house.

They won't leave alive.

Suddenly, the alarm quiets, leaving me in deafening silence. I can hear Annika talking, probably to the security company.

I hear shuffling coming from Richard's old office.

"Motherfucker," I whisper and quietly make my way down the hall, peeking around the doorjamb.

I move fast, and with one strike, I have the asshole on the floor. He lashes out, a taser in his hand, but he's no match for my strength. I turn the taser on him, and while his body convulses from the jolt, I haul him into a nearby chair and press my nose to his.

"I'm going to end you, asshole."

"Rafe?"

"Shit." I don't know if anyone else is in the house.

"Do we need the police?"

"No."

Annika tells the operator that everything is fine and hangs up.

"Get in here," I command and clench my jaw when her eyes widen at the sight of the man in the chair. "I need rope."

"Uh, will my robe sash do?"

"Sure." She passes it to me, and I get the jerk's hands tied behind his back just as he starts to come to. "I'm calling Carmine and Shane. Close and lock that door. I don't know if anyone else is here, and I won't leave you."

She does as I ask as I call my brothers.

"I could sue you," the jerk in the chair says. I punch him in the face.

"I suggest you shut the fuck up."

"Sue me?" Annika demands. "*Sue* me? For what? I didn't invite you here. You're trespassing, you moron. Just what the fuck do you think you're going to sue me for?"

He doesn't answer, just keeps his face lowered toward the floor.

"Carmine and Shane will scout the outside and clear the rest of the house. They're on their way."

"It's four in the morning," she says with a frown.

"Yeah, and we have an intruder."

Annika flips on some lights and sits on the leather couch, clenching her robe around her. Less than ten minutes later, there's a knock.

"All clear," Shane calls out. I hurry over and open the door to find Shane, Ivie, Carmine, and Nadia all standing on the other side.

"It's a party," I say dryly. "And this guy crashed it."

Nadia walks over to him, takes his chin in her fingers, and raises his face to hers. "Hello there, fucker. How does it feel to know you're about to die?"

"Fuck you, bitch."

"Now, see, I don't like that word." Nadia purses her lips in a pout and then backhands him with the butt of her weapon.

"That's MacDonald," Ivie says, narrowing her eyes. "This is the idiot who left the envelope yesterday."

"Back for more?" I ask him, but Annika approaches and looks into MacDonald's face.

"You were the waiter," she says, shaking her head. "*You* were the waiter at the wedding who gave me the first envelope."

He doesn't reply. He doesn't flinch. Gives no reaction at all.

I glance at Carmine and then Shane. This isn't the

first time someone infiltrated a wedding. I'm getting damn sick and tired of it.

"Who do you work for?" Annika asks.

Again, no reaction.

"Here, step back, babe." Annika does as I ask, and I plant the business end of my fist in the asshole's nose.

Blood gushes everywhere. He hisses a breath through his teeth.

"I'm about to start pulling off your fingernails," Shane says calmly as he pulls a pair of plyers out of his bag. "So, I suggest you start talking."

"Bullshit," MacDonald sneers.

Carmine unties him, holds one arm, and I take the other as Shane steps forward and plucks a nail right off his thumb.

"Son of a bitch!" MacDonald screams. "You're fucking crazy!"

"No...angry," I reply. "There's so much more that can be done to you before we let you die. You have no idea. You're going to want to talk."

"Who do you work for?" Annika asks again.

"I can't tell you that," MacDonald says, so Shane takes another nail. "I can't! If I do, they'll hurt my family."

"*We'll* hurt your family if you don't," Carmine replies. "Kind of a rock and a hard place, isn't it? If you rat them out, people get hurt. If you don't, people still get hurt. Either way, you're dead. Thing is, we're the ones dishing out the pain right now."

Shane takes another nail.

"The McCarthys," he wails.

I step back and shake my head. "The crime family in Boston?"

"Irish mafia," Carmine mutters.

"I'm just an errand-runner. I don't ask questions, and they don't tell me dick."

"Not a good place to be in, MacDonald," Nadia says. "Why Annika?"

"Like I said—" This time, Shane just breaks a finger. "Goddamn it! I don't know! I was told to deliver stuff to her."

"What were you doing inside her house tonight?" I ask. "Trying to deliver something in person?"

"No." He's weeping now. "I was supposed to take her."

"Take. Her. Where?" My face is inches from his now. His haunted eyes meet mine.

"To Boston. I overheard something about sex trafficking. They thought they could get more for her because she's willing to do...things." The last word is whispered. "That's all I know. I can take you to the boss. To Connor McCarthy. He's behind it all. Maybe you don't have to kill me if I help you out, right?"

"Wrong."

Shane pulls the wire from under his palm and wraps it around MacDonald's neck, then pulls until the life leaves the man's body before letting go.

"I'll call for cleanup," Carmine says, reaching for his phone.

"I'll make sure the jet is ready to go," I add.

"You're not going without me," Annika announces. We all turn to her. Her chest is heaving, and she looks like she wants to throw up.

She's not used to this. She's worked hard to make sure that *this* isn't part of her life.

"Every time one of these girls says that, it never turns out well," I say, shaking my head.

"If I stay here like some coward, you'll have to stay with me. To *protect* me," she points out. "Are you going to stand there and say that that idea is okay with you? That you're content to sit here with me while these four run off and kill the assholes responsible for this?"

I blow out a breath. "No. I can't say I'd be okay with it. But if that's what I have to do, then so be it."

"No." She's pacing now, absolutely pissed off. It's a sight to behold with her fiery blue eyes and mussed blond hair. "Absolutely not. If what he said is true, these fuckers thought they could *use* me. For sex. And why? Because they think I was a willing participant in *anything* that happened in those photos? Jesus, people saw me cry and beg. And no one did anything."

"Then that wasn't a reputable club, and was likely part of the sex trafficking epidemic, as well," Carmine says, fire shooting from his eyes. "Because real lifestyle clubs would never permit that. Ever."

"They're all going to pay," Annika says and turns

back to me. Her mind is made up. I've never seen her this...fierce.

It's a fucking turn-on.

"I want to look them in the eyes and know that it's because they ever fucked with me that they're going to die. That they hurt *any* woman, or anyone at all for that matter, and made them do things against their will. It's going to stop. Right now."

"Looks like we're all going to Boston," Ivie says with a grin. "And we're going to kick some ass."

We've cleared out of the office where the body is, and are sitting in the living room when the call comes in from Nadia's father.

"Papa?" Nadia frowns over at Annika. "Is everything okay? What? Wait, hold on, I'm putting you on speaker."

She taps her screen.

"Okay, you're on speaker. I'm here with everyone, including Annika. There was just an...issue at her place. But it's been handled."

"Firefly? Are you safe?"

"Yes, Uncle," Annika replies. "We're all okay. What's going on with you?"

"I just got off the phone with Carlo. We just got word that Thomas Luccio, the Chicago boss, and his family were found dead late last night."

"In their home?" I ask.

"No. At the bottom of the river. Luccio, his wife, and both grown children all had cement shoes on. We don't know what the motive was or who did it, but when these things happen, we all pay attention. I want you all to keep your eyes open."

"Pop's calling me," Carmine says and leaves the room to take the call. "Yeah, we're speaking to Igor now."

"We're headed to Boston," Nadia tells her father. "We have some business to see to there. I need you to know that we'll be leaving some blood behind, Papa. The McCarthys have been fucking around with Annika, and we're going to make them pay."

He's quiet for a long moment.

"Why wasn't I apprised of this situation?"

"Because we didn't know until about twenty minutes ago that it was them. Now that it's been confirmed, we're going in."

"Understood. Do what you need to do. But get in and out quickly. The McCarthys aren't particularly powerful, but we don't need a war."

"Agreed. It'll be quiet. No mess. I love you, Papa."

"I love you, too. All of you, stay safe."

He ends the call, and Nadia tucks her phone away.

"I'm going up to get dressed. I'll be ready in thirty," Annika says. I follow her up the stairs to her room. "You don't have to babysit me while I get dressed, Rafe."

"Do you understand what's about to happen?"

"Perfectly."

"Killing a man—"

"Look. I know that I've always stayed out of the family business, and I prefer it that way. And I also know that I haven't been the strongest of the group the past few days. But, damn it, Rafe, I'm pissed. And I have Tarenkov blood running through my veins. I know exactly what this means, what I'm getting myself into, and what I'll see when we get there. I'm going all the same."

I blow out a breath as she lets the robe fall to the floor, and with her blue eyes on mine, slips out of her nightgown, unashamed of her nudity. I've seen her naked more times than I can count. I know her body better than I know mine.

But I think, in this moment, I'm seeing more than just her body. She's naked in *every* way possible.

And she's trusting me to keep her safe and to help her see this through.

I'll be damned if I fail her.

CHAPTER 6

~ANNIKA~

"We go in quietly," Shane says as he briefs us all on the plane, just minutes from touching down in Boston. "There's going to be security. Rocco and I will take care of them before we go into the house."

"Why don't we go to the office?" I ask.

"Because we can't guarantee that McCarthy will be there," Carmine adds.

"It'll be the middle of the day with the time difference by the time we get there," Nadia says. "We can't guarantee that he'll be home, either."

"She has a point," Rafe says. "Half of us should go to the house, the other half to the office."

"No, we need to stick together," Shane insists. "If you'd like to try the office first, we can do that. We can go in as if we just want to have a meeting with

McCarthy. Make it seem like we're just a family visiting another's territory."

"I like that better," Nadia says. "It makes more sense and is way less messy."

"It's decided, then," Carmine says. They all check their weapons, even Ivie. I know that after everything she went through just a couple of months ago, she's become proficient in handling a gun as well as in hand-to-hand combat. She's a total badass.

But it's still surprising to see my best friend with a handgun.

Of course, I'm not armed. I could use one if I had to, but it's been so long that it's probably not wise for me to be armed.

"You stay with me," Rafe says quietly beside me. "You don't hesitate to move when I do. You stick with me as if you're fucking tied to me."

"Okay."

He nods as the airplane descends.

I know this is what both the Martinellis and my family do, but I've never witnessed it. It's fascinating to watch all of the people I trust more than anything transform from my easy-going, funny friends to stone-cold killers.

There's not much to say as we land. A large, black SUV waits for us near the plane. Rafe opens the front passenger-side door for me as everyone climbs in, and then Rafe joins me in the front, taking the driver's seat.

"I have it pulled up," Shane says as his phone starts giving us directions to the McCarthy office.

It takes about an hour to snake our way through traffic.

"You have to be fucking kidding me," Rafe growls as he pulls in behind an ambulance. Cops and another ambulance block the street, their lights flashing.

"What's going on?"

"I don't know." Carmine rolls down his window and waves to one of the police officers. "Hi there. We have an appointment with Mr. McCarthy in this building."

"Not today, you don't," the cop replies.

"Well, I guess we'll try to meet with him somewhere else, then."

"Nah, man. McCarthy's dead. I can't tell you more than that, except it sounds like he was into some bad shit."

"Well, damn." Carmine shakes his head. "Thanks for the information. We'll get out of your way."

Rafe puts the vehicle in reverse and, within seconds, we're driving away from the scene.

"I'm making some calls," Carmine says as he taps his phone. We listen to his side of the conversation, and when he hangs up, he drags his hand down his face. "Sounds like McCarthy has been threatening more than Annika. He was in deep with a sex trafficking ring, pissed off more people than he could count, and someone finally killed him early this morning."

"Beat us to it," Rafe says grimly. "Fucking pisses me off."

"At least, he's dead," Nadia says.

"I guess we're headed back to Denver," Ivie adds.

KNOWING that the asshole responsible for my harassment is gone and can't do it to anyone else is a relief. And yet, the trip was oddly anticlimactic.

We're in the plane again, headed back home. Ivie and Shane have their heads together at a table, talking low and intimately.

Carmine and Nadia sit on the couch across from me, both quiet. Carmine's reading on his iPad, and Nadia has her eyes closed, her head resting on her husband's shoulder.

They look cozy. Sweet.

In love.

I've had some bad moments of jealousy over the past several months when it comes to my cousin being able to marry the man she loves. After all, she fell in love with Carmine, the eldest son of Carlo Martinelli, and her father, *my* uncle, gave her his blessing to wed.

Though just over a decade ago, Uncle Igor made me leave Rafe behind because the Martinellis were not to be trusted and were off-limits for us.

Why did he make me break up with Rafe, someone I loved so much? We weren't hurting anyone. And then, so many years later, allow his daughter to marry the eldest of the Martinelli sons?

It feels...*wrong.*

I shift my gaze to Rafe, only to find him watching me with calm, blue eyes. He sips his coffee, lounging in his seat, his gray Henley shirtsleeves pushed up on his forearms where muscles twitch and move as he takes another sip from his white mug.

I want him. I want him more than anything in the world. Always have. I was once told that it was impossible because of our family trees.

Obviously, things have changed there. Nadia has Carmine, and Ivie has Shane. It's true that Ivie isn't related to us by blood, but she's as much a part of the Tarenkov family as I am.

Holding Rafe's gaze, I take a deep breath.

Yes, I want him. And while I may be damaged goods, I have to at least try to be with him damn it.

"THANKS FOR THE RIDE HOME," I say as I unlock the door and let us into the big, horrible house that I still live in. "I appreciate it. I'm sorry we all had to go so far just to find out that someone beat us to the punch."

"Don't be sorry," Rafe says. "Stay down here. I'm going to do a quick sweep of the house to make sure everything is secure."

"I'm sure—"

"Just please stay here," he says again and takes off up the stairs.

I blow out a breath and hurry over to the liquor cabinet, pouring myself a shot of vodka and slinging it back. I need some liquid courage for what I'm about to do. God, I'm nervous. I've always been able to say anything to Rafe. Anything at all. But something tells me he's not prepared for what's about to come out of my mouth.

"It looks like nothing has been disturbed since we left," he says as he hurries down the steps.

"Am I too damaged for you to love me?" I blurt out, needing to just get the words out of my head.

He stops cold and stares at me with wide eyes. "Excuse me?"

"You heard me. After everything that's happened, you know exactly what I went through with that idiot I refuse to name. And now that you know, are you disgusted? Does it ruin everything we might have been to each other?"

"No." He crosses to me and drags his knuckles down my cheek. "No, honey. What happened wasn't your fault. When you cried out in your sleep, and I came to your room...God, was that just last night? Anyway, when you talked in your sleep, it nearly tore my heart out. You said you were damaged goods and that I'd never love you."

"Yeah." I blow out the breath I've been holding. "That doesn't shock me."

"You're the most loveable person I've ever met, A." He leans in closer. My heart is pounding so hard I'm surprised he can't feel it.

Finally, after the longest one-point-five seconds ever, his lips meet mine in the softest, sweetest kiss of my life.

But before he can take it further, I plant my hand on his chest and push.

"Okay, I'm getting mixed signals here, Annika."

"I'm sorry." I clench my eyes shut and swallow hard. "That's not what I mean to do. It's not that I don't want you to kiss me."

"Good." He steps forward, but I put my hand up once more.

"But I can't do this here." I can't help but reach out for him. I press my palm to his chest and feel his heart beating as quickly as mine. It gives me the courage to keep talking. "This house is full of horrors that I'll never tell you about, Rafe. I just can't. I don't want those images in your mind. But at the same time, I don't want to start something new with you, something really great, while in this awful house."

"Looks like we need to go house hunting, then." His lips twitch. "Do you want to call your realtor, or do you want me to?"

"What? Like *today*?"

"No time like the present. It's only three in the afternoon. We can look at some places."

I shake my head, but his eyes are completely serious.

"You want to go house hunting. With me. Today."

"Yes."

I laugh but reach for my phone.

"Okay, let's do it."

"I WAS SO happy that you called," Noreen, my real estate agent says with a grin. "Some new condos came on the market this week. And there's a gorgeous townhouse I want to show you, as well."

"We're not in a hurry," I assure her. "So, we'll look at all of them if you have the time."

"I certainly do." Noreen winks and directs Rafe to park on the street in front of a brand-new condo building in downtown Denver. "As you can see, this is a new build. There are two and three-bedroom units with a four-bedroom penthouse unit still for sale, as well."

"I'd like to see the three-bedroom. And the penthouse."

"Perfect." She smiles widely and escorts us inside. "The three-bedroom I'm about to show you doesn't have to be the unit you go with. It's just ready for walk-throughs. There are other same-sized units with better views—for a bit higher price, of course."

"Of course." I nod and follow her inside. Denver is

damn expensive. Much more so than when I first moved here for my residency. But I like it here. My business is here. So, I'll pony up a lot for a condo.

It's a good thing that godforsaken house will bring in a nice amount of money.

"It's spacious," I say as I walk through the modern kitchen, complete with the farm sink I've always wanted. "And full of light."

"Yes, these condos have been decorated beautifully," Noreen says. "I'm going to go up to the penthouse to get it ready for you. Feel free to look around."

"Thanks."

Noreen leaves, and I turn to Rafe. "Well? What do you think?"

"It's your place, A."

I shrug a shoulder and look around the room, taking in the fireplace. The balcony. "Let's look at the bedrooms. I need a guest room and an office."

I walk down one hallway and find two good-sized bedrooms, each with its own bath. Then I retrace my steps and take the other hallway, which leads to the master.

"Wow, this is bigger than I expected."

"That's what she said," Rafe murmurs as he walks up behind me, wraps his arms around my waist, and kisses my neck.

It takes me so off guard that I spin and push back.

"What are you doing?"

"Trying it out."

"Trying *what* out?"

"The bedroom." He moves to me, and his hands glide from my hips to the small of my back as he pulls me close and nibbles my ear. My God, I might just slither down into a pile of goo at this man's feet.

He was always good at this. But was he *this* good, or did I just block it out of my memory? Because holy Christ on a cracker, the man can kiss.

"Well?"

"Well, what?"

He grins. "Does it feel *right* here?"

I want to tell him that it feels right everywhere, but Noreen calls out from the kitchen before I can.

"Annika? Are you still here?"

"In the master," I call back, my eyes on Rafe's. "It's a spacious unit."

"Yes, the square footage is well worth the price tag." Noreen grins. "Shall we go up to the penthouse?"

"Sure."

We follow Noreen through the condo and into the elevator. Rafe and I are at the back of the car while Noreen pushes the button.

Rafe slips his hand into mine, laces our fingers, and gives me a squeeze.

I want to cry in relief. God, I've missed him.

Soon, we arrive on the top floor, and when the doors slide open, we follow Noreen into the space.

"Wow," I breathe as we step inside.

"It's twice the square footage as the unit you just walked through," Noreen begins.

"And twice the price," I murmur but cross to the floor-to-ceiling windows to stare at the mountains to the west. "The view is incredible."

"One of the best in the city," Noreen agrees.

I turn to Rafe, but he's not looking at the mountains. He's watching me.

"Feel free to wander around," Noreen says and sits on the sofa. "I'll just answer some emails here and give you some privacy. If you have any questions, I'm here."

"Thank you."

We walk through the spacious unit. I like the bedrooms and bathrooms. Laundry. And when I walk into the master closet, I almost have an orgasm from all of the space.

"Wow."

"They always get you with the closets," Rafe says with a grin. "It's a hell of a closet."

"You're not kidding. But, damn, the price on this place is ridiculous."

"Denver is expensive," he says.

"Yeah."

And when I walk out to the bedroom and stand at the window to take in more of the views of the mountains, he does what he did at the last place. He steps up behind me, rests his hands on my shoulders, and lowers his lips to my neck.

How is it possible that my body can spring to life

with just the simplest touch from this man? It doesn't matter where we are—this or any other room. His touch will forever make me burn.

"What do you think?" he asks.

"It's not right. The house, not you."

He kisses me once more, then turns me to face him. "Are you determined to stay here in Denver?"

"My business is here." But the statement isn't firm; it's more conversational. "I'd rather not close it. I have employees I would hate to lay off."

"I understand that." He nods thoughtfully. "But a lot of things have changed for you. Have you given any thought to Seattle?"

I blink and frown. "No, honestly, I haven't. But Nadia will be there more. And probably Ivie, as well."

"You're wounding my ego, sweetheart."

I laugh. "Right. But, yes. You, too. Maybe moving to a new city and not just a new house is the fresh start I need. But my business…"

"There's no need to make any big decisions right away." He takes my face in his hands. "It's just something to think about. Talk to Ivie about it."

I love that he knows that I'll need to bounce this off my best friend.

He always *knows.*

"You're right. I'm in no hurry. And I'll think about it."

CHAPTER 7

~ANNIKA~

"I can't even begin to tell you how good it feels to have a girls' night that doesn't involve the mafia," I say as I pour us each a glass of wine. We're at Nadia's place in Denver, all in our leggings and baggy shirts, hair up in knots, looking way less than glamorous but incredibly comfortable.

"Every day involves the mafia," Nadia reminds me. "But it feels good to have things wrapped up and calm for once."

"And you get to go on your honeymoon tomorrow," Ivie adds, clinking her glass to Nadia's. "There's a tropical beach with your name written all over it."

"Thank the good Lord and all of the saints," Nadia agrees and takes a sip of her wine. "I'm ready to sip fruity drinks and soak in some sunshine. And have all the honeymoon sex. I still can't believe I'm a married woman. It's absolutely ridiculous to me."

"Carmine is perfect for you," I remind her.

The grin that spreads over her face is full of satisfaction. "Yeah. He is. Okay, enough about me. How are you, honey?"

"Oh, I'm good." I wave her off, but both Ivie and Nadia narrow their eyes at me. "What? I am. I'm fine."

"Fine." Ivie nods and sips her wine. "You're fine."

"Yes. I'm fine."

"Bullshit. Spill it, Tarenkov."

I shake my head and laugh at my friends as I reknot my hair.

"Something's up with you," Ivie agrees.

"Okay." I take another sip of wine for courage. "I do have some stuff to talk through. And you guys are the only ones I can do that with."

"And we're right here," Nadia says.

"You know I'm selling the house."

"Thank God," Ivie says. "I hate that place."

"Me, too. I'm selling. Rafe and I went and looked at some condos the other day."

"You went without us?" Nadia demands. "Damn it, A, I love house hunting."

"But she went with *Rafe*," Ivie reminds her. "We would have been third wheels."

"Rafe isn't the point. I went, and nothing felt right. The thing is, I don't know if *Denver* feels right anymore. I've been here a long time, and I love it, but there's nothing here for me except the spa. And I love it, and people depend on me there, but it's just…"

"It doesn't fit anymore?" Nadia asks.

"Yeah. I think that's it. But that makes me feel so guilty because I have a staff of people who depend on me for their jobs. I can't just close it down."

"You're the boss," Ivie points out. "You can totally close it down."

"But you are my office manager."

"I am. And I like my job, but to be brutally honest, I also love working with Shane. I don't know, A, I think our lives are starting to change a bit. And it's for the better. If you offer the other employees a severance package and a letter of recommendation, they'll be fine. It's all in how you handle the situation. There are so many medi-spas here in Denver, and they're all wonderful employees. They won't have a problem finding something else."

I bite the inside of my cheek, thinking it over. "Do you really think so?"

"I do." She nods and reaches over to lay her hand over mine. "I think you're an awesome person for being worried about it. But don't overthink it. You need to do what's right for you."

"If you sell everything here and move, where do you want to go?" Nadia asks.

"Well, Rafe suggested Seattle."

My two best friends beam at me, and I feel my cheeks flush.

"So, it *is* about Rafe," Nadia says smugly.

"This part could be," I admit. "I'm a complete basket

case, you guys. I have gone from thinking that I can never be with the man, that I'm not good enough, to saying '*fuck it*,' all in a matter of *hours*."

"Fuck the wine," Nadia says as she stands. "We need tequila."

She quickly returns with a full bottle, three shot glasses, and a baggie full of cut-up limes.

"Forgot the salt," she says before rushing to the kitchen to fetch the shaker.

"Mixing wine and tequila doesn't sound like a good idea," I say with a frown.

"Live a little," Nadia suggests and pours the shots. "And keep talking."

"I'm so back and forth, and it's confusing me. I mean, all we've done is kiss, but it made me feel exactly the way I did all those years ago, you know?"

"No, I don't know, because you didn't tell me about it before, remember?" Nadia takes a shot and scowls at me as she sucks on a lime. "I can't believe you didn't tell me."

"I didn't want Uncle Igor to find out," I admit quietly. "But he found out anyway, and made me break up with him. Because he was a Martinelli."

"He's still a Martinelli," Ivie points out.

"Yeah, but things have changed quite a bit from what they were a decade ago," Nadia points out. "I don't think you'll have a problem with the family this time around."

I nod, thinking it over.

"I like that he suggested Seattle," Ivie says. "Nadia and I will be there more often now, and maybe it's the right time for you to start over somewhere new."

"That's what I'm thinking." I blow out a breath. "Change is scary, you know?"

"No, it's exciting," Nadia says. "It's the chance for a fresh start, and you already have a support system there. You can always open a new spa in Seattle, or just take your time and think about what you want."

"Actually, that's a good question," Ivie adds. "What *do* you want, A? In a perfect world, what do you see happening for yourself?"

I take a shot, then suck on a lime. "I want Rafe," I admit. "God, I want him."

"Then I think you've already decided," Ivie says with a wide smile. "And I'm so excited for you, friend."

"Me, too. I have Noreen the realtor coming to the house tomorrow so we can put it on the market. I really don't want to spend any more nights there."

"Stay here," Nadia offers, gesturing to her beautiful Denver home. "Carmine and I leave tomorrow. You'll have the place to yourself."

"Really? You don't think Carmine would mind?"

"Honey, Carmine is a softy when it comes to women. All of our men are. He knows your situation. He'll be absolutely fine with you staying here."

"They're good people." I look down into my empty shot glass, and Nadia fills it back up. "The guys. They're good. And I'm really so glad they're ours. Well, I don't know for sure about Rafe being mine, but you know what I mean."

"No man looks at a woman the way Rafe looks at you and doesn't consider her his," Nadia replies, her blue eyes solemn. "And, yes, they're good. I mean, they kill people and stuff, but they're good men."

I laugh and then nod. "Good killers. I guess it's a thing."

"It's totally a thing." Nadia holds her glass up for us to clink. "To the sexy Martinelli men."

"And their gorgeous women," Ivie adds just before we all shoot the tequila.

"You know, Ivie, I love the confidence that has grown in you since you started fucking Shane," Nadia says. "It's high time you realize just how beautiful and wonderful you are."

"Thanks." She smiles shyly. "It's hard to continue thinking of yourself as dowdy and as the ugly duckling when the man you love can't keep his hands off you and tells you how irresistible you are all the time."

"I like Shane a lot," I say and bring my knees up to my chest. "He's really intense and quiet, but I can see how much he loves you. And I know, without a doubt, that you're safe with him."

"We're all safe," Ivie says. "And it's a damn good feeling."

∾

I CAN HANDLE THE HANGOVER. It's the memories that hurt.

I blow out a breath, prop my hands on my hips, and try not to think about how horribly I must smell right now. I stayed the night at Nadia's, and after she and Carmine left for their fun honeymoon this morning, I dragged my ass out of their house and over to mine so I could pack up what I want to keep.

So far, it's two boxes.

In the three hours that I've been here, I've managed to throw away a ton of crap. I've made piles of things to be donated. And all of the furniture can also be donated or sold with the house.

Thankfully, Richard and I only lived here for a few months before he died, so I don't have many years' worth of accumulation to dig through. I've managed to pack a couple of bags full of clothes to last me several weeks, all of my toiletries, and I have my briefcase full of office stuff. I can be mobile for a little while.

With my closet emptied, I make my way downstairs. I want to keep my KitchenAid mixer. It was a gift from Ivie, and I use it a lot. I like to cook. I also box up the cookware that was a wedding gift, only because it was exactly what I wanted when I registered, and it's top-of-the-line. I also throw a few knickknacks into the box, but the rest can go.

Next, I box up my library. This was my favorite room in the house, and a space that Richard never came into. He didn't like to read. It takes more than an hour to box the books because I like to look at each one and think about how much I love the stories inside.

But once the shelves are empty, I only have two rooms left to tackle, and I've been avoiding them both like the plague.

Richard's office, and the basement.

I gather up a couple of empty boxes and walk into the office first.

Thankfully, right after he died, we went through most of the paperwork left in here, and I burned it in the backyard while I guzzled down a bottle of wine. Most of what's here is just masculine furniture and some office supplies.

I start to box up some things but then stop and sit back on my haunches.

"What am I packing anything for?" I wonder aloud. "So it can sit in a storage closet until I die and become someone else's problem? That's dumb. I don't want any of this."

I leave it all in the middle of the room, set to go out in the trash. I do make sure there's nothing in there that should be shredded, but it all looks pretty harmless.

Until I cross to the safe behind a painting on the wall. I already looked inside after he died, and it was empty, but I open it one last time just to make sure I didn't overlook anything.

"Empty," I murmur, staring at the black velvet interior. But just as I'm about to turn to leave, I notice a small, black ribbon in the back corner. "I swear my life is a movie plot."

I close my eyes and pinch the bridge of my nose.

"I don't want to pull on that ribbon." I shake my head, pace the room, and then come back to the safe. "But I have to. Goddamn you, Richard."

I tug on the little strip of fabric, and a false wall gives way. Behind it is a stack of cash at least six inches thick and an envelope with my name on it.

"Fuck fuck fuck fuck fuck."

I take it all to the ugly brown couch and sit, then open the envelope. With dread hanging heavy in my belly, I begin to read.

Annika,

If you're reading this, you found the hidden compartment in the safe. You'd better hope that I'm dead. Because if not, and I find out you've been snooping, I'll kill you myself.

Now, then. In the event that I've died, there are a few things to say. First of all, our marriage is a scam. I don't love you. I find you to be the most boring and inconvenient person I've ever met in my life. You're a snooze-fest, A. But I know your heart is in the right place, and that since we've been married, I've put you in situations that you found to be...uncomfortable.

I have to put the letter down and take a deep breath so I don't rip it to shreds before I'm finished reading.

Uncomfortable? Motherfucker.

While you were a means to an end for me, I know that you entered into our marriage with the best of intentions, and that you did love me. I'm not so heartless that I don't recognize that. Because I couldn't return your love, and to thank you for your loyalty and dedication, I've stashed some money away for you. There is a quarter of a million dollars here for you. I know that's not much compared to what your family has at its disposal, but it's what I can offer you, along with the money you'll get from the sale of this horrible house.

Be well, Annika.

R

I blow out a breath, fold the note, and tuck it back into the envelope, then into my back pocket. So, he left me with a bunch of money and a lot of regret.

Generous of him, really.

I roll my eyes, take the money out of the safe, and then pause when I see a small scrap of paper.

It's just a phone number.

I tuck it away and, more than ready to be done with this room, walk out.

Now I just have to tackle the basement, which is really the root of my hate for this home, and for the man I lived with here.

But there's no way in hell that I'd allow someone else to deal with what's down there. It's too humiliating. Too horrible.

I would take a swig of liquor, but I'm still hungover from last night. Instead, I take a long drink of water and square my shoulders.

I flip on the stairway lights and feel the ball of dread

grow in my stomach with each step until it feels like it might suffocate me.

When I reach the bottom and turn on the lights, it's just…empty. There's no sign that anything used to be down here at all. No wall of whips and restraints. No bed. No toys.

Nothing.

I blink, sure I'm imagining things. I haven't been down here since before Richard died. I certainly haven't let anyone else come down here.

Where did it all go?

"Annika?"

I turn and hurry up the stairs at the sound of Noreen's voice.

"Oh, there you are," she says with a smile. "What's wrong? You look like you've seen a ghost."

"Oh." I shake my head and force a smile to my lips. "Nothing. It's just already been a long day."

"I understand. Selling a house is a lot of work. And I see you've been hard at it. I'm glad we've already taken photos for the listing."

"Yeah." I cringe. "I'll get this cleaned up. I won't be living here anymore, so I wanted to clear some stuff out. I have a dumpster coming for the trash, and I'm donating a bunch of things to charity. The rest can be sold with the house if the buyer wants it."

"We can take care of that," Noreen assures me. "Do you have somewhere to go?"

"Yes, several somewheres, actually. I'll be okay."

"Good. Okay, let's do a walk-through, and I'll put the sign in the yard. It'll go up online this afternoon. It's a seller's market right now, so I don't think it'll sit for long."

"Perfect. The sooner we can sell, and I can wipe my hands of it, the better."

CHAPTER 8

"My house sold in three days."

Annika's voice in my ear is like a balm to my soul. I've been staying away, letting her sort through everything she needs to figure out. I want to be there, helping her. Hell, I want to handle everything for her and protect her from any more pain.

But I know Annika. She needs to handle this on her own.

"It actually went into a bidding war, and I got more than the asking price," she continues. "I was stunned. And then, when I had the meeting with everyone at the clinic and told them my plans, they were so sweet about it. There were some tears and hugs, but they all understood."

"I'm sure you offered them a nice severance package."

Her chuckle makes me grin. "Of course. It didn't

hurt. I closed the clinic immediately and referred my existing patients to other doctors."

"You're wrapping it up quickly."

"Yeah." She's quiet for a moment.

"Did I lose you?"

"No, I—" She sighs. "Can I come see you in Seattle for a while?"

Her words come out in a quick whoosh of air, and the insecurity in her voice makes me frown.

"I've been waiting for you to do what you need to, A. You're always welcome to be with me, no matter where I am. When would you like to come?"

"It's Wednesday now, and Ivie is here helping me close up the spa. We should be done by Saturday. How does Sunday work for you?"

"What time do you want to leave?"

"Oh, I thought I'd just book a flight and you could pick me up at the airport."

"I'll come get you. I'll bring the plane myself so it's just the two of us. You can be my co-pilot."

"Is that safe?"

I laugh, excited at the thought of having her here with me in just a few days. "Okay, there may be three of us on the plane. I just have to tell you, I'm so proud of you, Annika."

"For what? Being an adult?"

"Yes, actually. And for handling everything in that classy way you always do. Seattle will be lucky to have you."

Hell, *I'll* be lucky to have her.

But I don't want to move too fast or scare her away. I just need her with me. And it's going to happen, sooner than expected.

"Well, I'll just be happy and relieved when all of this is settled and all I have to do is come back to sign closing papers in about a month. I'm getting there. So, I'll see you Sunday?"

"Absolutely. Make sure you're eating, okay? And getting rest. I know you, and you'll work yourself into exhaustion."

"Yes, sir." She chuckles again. "I'm eating. Sleeping so-so. It'll get better. I'd better go. Ivie's giving me the stink eye because she's carrying boxes, and I'm flirting with you on the phone."

"Well, I guess we can't have her giving you the stink eye. I'll be in touch. Call me if you need anything at all, okay?"

"Okay, thank you. See you soon."

She clicks off. I set the phone down and stare out the windows at the city of Seattle as it buzzes down below.

I've kept a condo in the building my family owns for several years. I've never felt the need to buy a house that I have to maintain the way Carmine does. He likes being out of town.

He's very much like our late grandmother in that respect.

Shane and I have been content with our condos in

our building. But Shane is rarely here, preferring to spend his time at his ranch in the mountains of Colorado.

I've always felt that I'm in limbo. Missing something. I didn't know what I was missing exactly, until now.

Annika.

My life isn't complete without her. This condo has been fine for me because I didn't have her with me to make a home.

But that's about to change. I know I need to be patient, to take it slowly, but once I have her with me again, I'm never letting her go.

This time, it'll be forever.

"I'M GOING to get Annika in the morning," I say to my father as we sit in his office, finishing up some business.

"And where are you taking her?" he asks.

"I'm bringing her here, to Seattle. She sold the house and closed her business."

He raises an eyebrow. "Planning to marry her, are you?"

I hold my father's gaze. "Yes, eventually. For now, she needs a new start, and I suggested Seattle. Especially now that Nadia and Ivie will be here more often. It seemed like a good choice for her."

"Not to mention, *you've* been in love with her for years."

I blink in surprise, and my father laughs.

"I don't know why my children all think I'm blind and oblivious to what's going on. I'm not, you know. I knew why you stayed at that college all those years. So did Igor. We were not friends then."

"No." I clench my jaw and have to make myself keep my hands loose. "You weren't."

"Things change. People grow. Igor may be the only man in the world who understands my life and the pressures that go with it. We've had our ups and downs but have grown to trust and respect each other. We wouldn't allow our families to tie themselves to each other if it were any other way, and you know that."

"Yes." I nod once. "I know that."

"And you're bitter that Carmine married Nadia after you were torn from Annika all those years ago."

I stand and pace my father's office, feeling the frustration bubbling up. "I don't mean to feel that way, and it's not something I think about every day, but yes. I guess so. The game changed, and Carmine is with a great woman that he loves very much. I wanted the same."

I turn back to find my father watching me with speculative eyes.

"I *want* the same."

"Well, when the time comes, if Annika is agreeable, you won't get any pushback from me, son. She's a beautiful woman who didn't deserve what happened to her. You know your mother and I will welcome her into the family the way we've done with Nadia and Ivie."

"I know." I sit again and smile softly. "Mom's over the moon, you know?"

"All of her boys have found their match. It means more people to love, babies to come. Your mother has a big heart."

"A ruthless one," I add.

"If need be, absolutely. We can't function in this life any other way, Rocco. But at the end of the day, family is everything. To your mother, and to me. And we'll do whatever we need to do to make sure that ours is protected and happy."

"I know. By any means necessary."

"Yes." His eyes take on that gleam I've always admired when it comes to his work. Carmine shares it. It's how I know that my eldest brother will make an excellent boss someday. "By any means necessary. Now, you go get your woman and bring her back here where we can keep her safe and let her heal."

"Yeah." I swallow. "She needs that. Pop, you know I like living in the condo."

"But?"

"But I don't think it's a long-term solution. If things with Annika work out, and I'm banking on them working out, she needs a *home*."

"You're right. What are you thinking?"

I shake my head, thinking it over. "I don't know yet. I think it depends on her, you know?"

"You're a smart man, my boy." He laughs a little, his broad shoulders shaking. "Get her here and get settled. She'll know what she wants. Or, you'll decide together."

I nod. "You're right. I guess I'm just impatient after waiting so long for her."

"I would be, too. Did you know that your mother turned me down over and over again before we finally got together?"

"No. I thought you guys fell in love and got married six weeks later."

"That part is true, but she made me work for it for a long while. Anything worth having is worth the work and the wait."

"Annika's definitely worth it."

"Let me know when you get home. Your mother will want to invite you both over for dinner."

I grin. "Mom's turning into an even bigger mother hen than she was when we were little."

"She always wanted a girl," Pop says with a laugh. "Now that she's getting some, she's beside herself. Humor her, will you?"

"Sure. You know I never pass up a free meal." I tap my knuckles on his desk and stand. "Thanks, Pop."

"Anytime. Be safe."

I nod, leave his office, press the button for the elevator, and ride it down to my condo. It's been cleaned from top to bottom and is ready for my girl.

I just have to fetch her.

WHY AM I SO NERVOUS? I feel like a kid on his first date.

I walk up to Carmine's door and knock. She must have been watching for me because she swings the door open and throws herself into my arms.

"You're here!"

"I said I would be." I kiss the top of her head and breathe in her citrus scent. "Are you ready?"

"Yes, everything's done. I just have to lock up the house for Nadia." She pulls back, flashes me that killer smile, and then rushes away to gather her bags and make sure everything is locked up tight. While she checks the windows, I haul her bags to the car and meet her at the door as she locks up and turns to me with a wide grin. "Let's get the hell out of here."

"You don't have to tell me twice."

I open the car door for her, then jump into the driver's seat and point us in the direction of the smaller airfield used for private use.

"It's so funny because less than two weeks ago, I planned to stay in Denver. And now that I've changed that plan, I can't wait to get out of here."

"You've worked hard the last few days."

"Yeah, I'm exhausted. But also energized. Does that make sense?"

"It does to me."

She reaches over and pats my arm. "Thanks for this. For everything."

"You don't have to thank me for anything."

"I do." She grins and bounces in the seat. "I'm ready for a new adventure."

"Well, that I can deliver."

"I'm still living in the condo," I inform Annika several hours later as I pull my Porsche into the parking garage under our building and park in my space. "It has a good view."

"It's going to be great," she assures me. "I'll help with the bags. They're all on wheels anyway."

Between the two of us, we manage to get everything upstairs in one trip. Once we muscle everything inside, Annika takes a deep breath and soaks everything in.

"Oh, Rafe, this is *nice.*"

She walks into the kitchen where she admires the deep sink, the gas stove, and runs her hand along the big island.

"I can cook so many great things in here."

"You always did cook well."

"I'm better now." She winks and saunters over to the windows. "You're right. This is a great view of the city. I can even see the water and watch the ferries float over the Sound."

"The sunset is beautiful." I shove my hands into my

pockets, feeling nervous all over again. I want to touch her, but I don't want to make her uncomfortable or move too fast.

"Let me show you the rest," I suggest and lead her through the living area to the bedrooms. "I only have the two bedrooms, but I think this is a comfortable space."

I don't mention that I had the guest room furnished last week and decorated to her tastes.

"Beautiful," she says with a nod.

"There's a bathroom right over here. That's all yours."

"Okay. Where's your room?"

"This way." I lead her down the hall to my bedroom and swallow hard. Jesus, just having her in my place is hard enough, but in my bedroom? How am I supposed to keep my hands to myself?

"This is huge," she says with a laugh and checks out my closet. "You don't have much in here. It looks empty."

"I'm a dude. I don't need much."

"All this space is just going to waste." She clucks her tongue and then pokes her head into the bathroom. "And look at that tub!"

"I can't complain about the tub," I agree and watch with a smile as she gets right into it, clothes and all, and lounges back as if she's taking it for a test drive.

"This is sweet."

"Like you."

Her grin turns soft as she gazes up at me. "Rafe?"

"Yeah?"

"What if I don't want to sleep in the guest room?"

I lean back on the vanity and cross my arms over my chest. "Well, I have a couch."

Her eyes fill with humor. "What if I want to sleep in *your* room?"

"I suppose that could work. Of course, that's where I sleep, so you'll have to share the bed with me."

She laughs and pulls herself up, then climbs out of the tub.

"That works for me." She crosses to me, takes my hands in hers, and tilts her lips up toward mine.

I never *could* resist this woman.

And now I don't have to.

I close my mouth over hers, gently sampling her. She tastes of the mint she had in the car, but more than that, she tastes of *Annika.* Like everything good in the world.

I lay my palm over her jaw, encompassing her neck and cheek, and take the kiss deeper, wanting to memorize every nuance. Each breath.

She sighs and leans into me, surrendering to me. Her breasts press against me, and I want to scoop her up and take her to bed—lose myself in her for several hours.

And I will.

Eventually.

"Rafe?"

"Yes, baby?"

"You kept asking me in those other condos if it felt right. If it was the place for me."

"I did."

"This is the one. Right here. This feels right."

I let out the breath I didn't know I'd been holding all day.

"I feel it, too."

Her smile is slow and full of pure female satisfaction. "Good."

CHAPTER 9

~ANNIKA~

*W*e didn't have sex. I thought we would the first night I was in his place, but it didn't happen. We ended up ordering in Chinese food and talked for hours, the way we used to when we were kids and falling in love.

That's not to say that just because we didn't do the deed, that he didn't touch me. No, Rafe is the king of physical affection. There was plenty of hand-holding and hair-playing. He kissed me some and traced his fingers down my cheek and over my jawline.

It's safe to say that he kept me in a constant state of pleasant arousal all day and into the evening.

And when we finally went to bed, we curled up together, fully clothed, and whispered into the night.

As much as I can't wait to get naked with this man, I have to admit that our first night together was exactly what I needed.

I stretch and roll over in bed, expecting to find Rafe next to me, but the bed is empty. And when I reach out to touch where he lay, the bedsheets are cool.

He's been up for a while.

I sit up, yawn, scratch my arm, and glance around. Rafe's place is nice. It's not fancy, and he certainly hasn't done much to make it look like anything but a bachelor pad, but it's super clean and updated. I can't wait to get my hands on that kitchen.

I shuffle sleepily into the bathroom with the best tub I've ever seen and consider taking a bath, when it occurs to me that I smell...*bacon.*

Is he making us breakfast?

I hurry through the condo to the kitchen and stop short at the sight that greets me.

Rafe, shirtless with a white towel flung carelessly over his shoulder. His skin is smooth and tanned, and the muscles beneath bunch as he moves from the stove to the mixing bowl on the countertop.

He's just so...*hot.* He's big, at well over six feet, with broad shoulders. But his movements are graceful. Those clever hands crack an egg into a bowl, and he gives it a whisk.

He's so competent in the kitchen, it's as if he makes breakfast every morning of the week.

When we were together before, he hated to cook.

This new side to him is...intriguing.

"Are you going to hover, or are you going to come

and get a cup of coffee?" he asks without turning around.

"I didn't make any noise. How did you know I was here?"

"I always know where you are, Annika." He turns to look at me over his shoulder, and the look he sends me makes my stomach quiver. "I hope you're hungry."

"Oh, I'm hungry." I cross to the island and sit in one of the stools, resting my chin in my hand as I watch while Rafe moves about with grace. I don't mention that I'm equally hungry for him to boost me up onto this island and have his way with me, as I am to get my fingers on that bacon. "Wait, you made bacon with no shirt on? That's awfully *brave* of you."

"No." He chuckles and then turns to pass me a cup of coffee, just the way I've always liked it. He remembers how I take my coffee? "I was wearing a shirt, but it got splattered, so I took it off."

He flips the pancakes.

"How do you want your eggs?"

"I have to say, I'm impressed, Rafe. You used to hate to cook."

"I can't eat takeout all the time like I could when I had the metabolism of a teenager," he replies. "And a man has to eat."

"I suspect your metabolism is just fine." I sip my coffee. "I'll take mine scrambled."

"Thank God. That's the only way I know to make them."

We laugh together as Rafe cracks more eggs into a clean bowl and begins whisking them with a fork.

"Did you know that if you add a little dill to the eggs, it adds a nice flavor?" I ask.

"Who's doing the cooking here?" He opens the spice cabinet and hums as he picks up little bottles and then sets them down again. "Dill is on the shopping list."

"We have a shopping list?"

"Of course. I didn't know what you might like to snack on. I remember some of the things you used to eat, but tastes change."

"Going to the store sounds good to me. I'd like to start cooking dinner in here tonight. Unless you have other plans."

"My mother invited us over for dinner." He sends me an apologetic glance. "But I can cancel if you'd like to take a couple of days to settle in first."

"I adore your mother," I reply honestly. "I can cook tomorrow. Ivie told me the other day that she and Shane are coming to Seattle for a couple of weeks. They arrive on Wednesday."

"Shane mentioned it," he replies as he sets my plate in front of me and then joins me with a loaded serving of his own. "It's been nice this fall. Not as rainy as usual. If the weather holds, we might take the boat out on the Sound."

"You have a boat?" I munch happily on a piece of bacon.

"A few, actually. My father always liked to sail. We

spent a lot of time on the water growing up. It's been a busy year, so we haven't been out as often as we'd like. If the weather holds, we'll go."

"Fun."

"Do you get seasick?"

"I never have." I shrug a shoulder. "I should be fine."

"Good." He leans over and kisses my temple. "I'm looking forward to sailing with you."

"So, let me get this straight. You're a badass mobster who cooks breakfast and enjoys sailing?"

"I'm a man of depth." He chuckles. "Mobsters have lives, too, you know."

"Sure. Those lives just include killing people."

"Sometimes." His voice quiets as he wipes his mouth. "Sometimes, it does. But that doesn't happen as often as you'd think. Certainly not as often as it has over the past year."

"You really have had a busy year, haven't you?"

"Yes." He laughs, and I can't help but join in. "It's nice to know that things are calming down a bit. At least, for a little while. It gives me time to spend with you."

"I have questions."

He cocks an eyebrow. "Okay. Shoot."

"I know that Carmine is a financial planner and works for the family."

"Yes. He's a nerd."

I smirk. "And Shane does stuff for the government that we're not really allowed to know about."

"Yes, he's a meathead."

I laugh and bump him with my shoulder. "Why don't I know what you do?"

"You know." He frowns over at me. "I fly."

"For who?"

"Anyone who wants to hire me. Although I have a stable of regulars that I work for and haven't taken on anyone new in quite some time."

I sit and blink at him. "I knew you know *how* to fly, it just didn't occur to me that you did it for a living."

"I'd rather fly than do just about anything else."

"Then why don't you work for a commercial airline?"

"Because I have a demanding family, and I need to be available to them at a moment's notice. That's hard to do when you're on a rotating schedule with an airline." He shrugs and shoves almost half of a pancake into his mouth. "I'm doing what I like."

"Do you enjoy working with the family?"

He swallows and seems to think it over. "I love my family. If I choose *not* to work with them, I'd have to leave. And that's not an option for me."

"I see."

He glances my way. "But you don't like that answer."

I push my empty plate aside and offer him a shrug. "I don't know what answer I want, to be honest. I love that you're close to your family. I'm close to mine, as well. But I've never wanted to be involved with the family business. And my uncle has always made me feel that he loves me whether I want to participate or not."

"It's not like you do nothing, Annika," he reminds me as he stands and puts the dirty dishes in the dishwasher. "I know for a fact that Igor has you handy in case someone needs to be patched up."

"I don't mind that," I admit softly. "And it doesn't happen often. I guess my point is, my uncle wouldn't disown me if I didn't want to help with the family business."

"I'm a man," Rafe says simply. I start to argue, but he holds up a hand. "Call it sexist or misogynistic, but it doesn't change the fact that if I were a woman, less would be expected of me. My father wouldn't disown me, but he would shut me out of a lot. I wouldn't be privy to information, and I certainly wouldn't have the protection I have now."

"And then there's the money," I say and know immediately by the look in his blue eyes that I've overstepped. "I'm sorry, I didn't mean—"

"My father isn't the only one in this room who's wealthy," he reminds me. "The last time I checked, you've never wanted for anything. Or gone without."

"Rafe, I didn't mean to insult you."

"Well, you did. I work my ass off for this family. I kill, I run all over this godforsaken globe, and I won't have you questioning my motives. I'm here because I *love* my family. If that's not something you want to be a part of, or if it's something you find insulting, we can find another place for you to stay."

"Jesus." I hang my head in my hands and wish I could hit the rewind button to go back about ten minutes. "I'm a bitch."

"Right now? Yeah."

My head snaps up. There's not only anger in his voice. There's hurt, as well, and it makes me feel like the worst person ever. "It came out entirely harsher than I meant, Rafe. All I meant was—you know what? It doesn't matter. I'm sorry. I was out of line. Nothing you could do would insult me, and I don't want to stay anywhere else."

He blows out a breath and hangs his head.

"Forget it. Let's get ready to do some sight-seeing before we go see my parents this evening."

He moves to walk past me, and I reach out for his hand, tugging him to me.

"I'm sorry."

"I said forget it."

I wrap my arms around his middle and hold on tightly. "I have a stupid mouth, and I didn't mean it."

"Hey." He kisses my head, and it makes me feel a little bit better. "I said it's okay. Maybe I just know that you never wanted to be involved with someone who's committed to the organization the way I am. I'm not leaving it, A. And you need to know that before we go much further."

"I know it." I look up at him. "I know, Rafe. And if I

thought I couldn't deal with it, I wouldn't be here. The truth is, I just want to be with you. No matter what."

He lets out a long breath and kisses my forehead.

"It's fine, Annika. Let's go have a good day."

"Okay."

"ARE YOU ENJOYING SEATTLE, DEAR?" Rafe's mother, Flavia Martinelli, asks me later that evening. "Have you been sight-seeing?"

"She just got here yesterday, Mom," Rafe says but wraps his arm around his mother's shoulders and gives her an affectionate squeeze.

"Well, we did do some sight-seeing today," I reply as Flavia fills my glass with wine. "Rafe took me to Pike Place Market, where he bought me the most amazing bouquet."

"The market really does have the best flowers," Flavia agrees.

"We wandered around downtown and just had a good day."

"And what do you think of the condo?" Carlo asks.

"It's a nice place." I smile politely and sit next to Rafe at the table, where appetizers are being served.

By staff.

I'm used to this at Uncle Igor's house, and I always forget how fancy it makes me feel until I'm in the situation again.

"I love the view," I continue. "The water is just *so* blue. And it's fun to watch the ferries float on the Sound, as well."

"It really is a nice view," Flavia agrees. "Perhaps you should buy a house near the water, Rafe."

I frown as I take a bite of my Caprese salad and turn to Rafe. "Are you looking for a house?"

"Well, you two can't live in the condo forever," Flavia continues. "It's so small. There's no room to stretch out and enjoy each other. And what about when you start having children? No, it certainly won't do for the long term. But I know of some absolutely *gorgeous* homes for sale that have amazing views. One of my good friends is a realtor. I'll give her a call next week."

"I don't think I'm in a rush to buy a house," Rafe says and eyes me warily. "I haven't even talked to Annika about it yet."

"Oh." Flavia looks between us and cringes. "Oh, dear. I'm sorry to speak out of turn. My mind just starts working, and my mouth starts to babble."

I smile, but I make a mental note to ask Rafe *many* questions when we get back to the condo. I feel like I'm missing something, something big. Like he isn't telling me everything.

And Flavia mentioned *children.* I don't know how I feel about kids. At least, kids of my own. I mean, I just got here.

We haven't even had sex yet, not to mention the fact

that we certainly haven't talked about anything long term.

I thought we'd take things slow. Because while it's a fact that I want to be with Rafe for the rest of my life, I'm still healing from a lot of garbage.

"Annika?"

I glance up and realize that Flavia asked me a question. "I'm sorry, I was too busy having a party in my mouth with this salad."

The other woman laughs and then nods. "It's my favorite, as well. I was just wondering if you've thought about opening another medi-spa here in Seattle. I'd love to be your first patient."

I grin at the thought. "Mrs. Martinelli, you're lovely without my help."

"Well, then, just think about what a knockout I'll be *with* your help."

We all laugh, and I feel much more comfortable as we settle in to enjoy each other's company.

CHAPTER 10

~RAFE~

I could kill my mother.

I shift gears manually and merge onto the freeway while Annika sits quietly next to me.

"My mom means well."

She turns her head towards me and offers me a smile in the darkness. "I adore your mom. She's sweet and fun."

"I wish she hadn't gone on and on about me buying a new house."

Annika shifts in her seat, facing me now. "I was going to ask about that. Do you want to move out of the condo? You hadn't mentioned it before."

I sigh deeply and rub my hand over my mouth as I keep my eyes on the freeway. It's late into the evening, so traffic is light.

"I'd only started thinking about it," I admit, not sure

how much to say. I don't want to scare her by talking about things that could happen in the long term. We aren't there yet. This is still new for both of us.

But damn it, I'm a planner.

"You don't like the condo?" she asks.

"I like it fine." I glance her way and find her watching me carefully. "It's convenient since it's downtown and only about twenty minutes from the airstrip."

"But?"

I shake my head with a chuckle. "I was just considering a house in a nice neighborhood. Maybe with a water view."

"When did you start thinking about this?"

I bite the inside of my cheek until I taste coppery blood on my tongue.

"About a week ago."

She's quiet for a long moment and then clears her throat. "Are you considering a house because of *me?*"

"I don't know." I blow out a breath. "Maybe. Look, I know that the condo isn't the best."

I take my exit off the freeway.

"I like the condo."

"It's small. No yard. And most of the building is used for business, so that's probably not something I'd like to have you living with for long."

"Rafe, you don't have to buy a whole house just because I'm staying with you for a little while."

I park in my space and turn to her with a scowl. "What do you mean, for a little while?"

Her mouth bobs open and closed, and then she simply sighs and closes her eyes. "I'm saying the wrong things."

"I think we're both doing a good job of that."

I jump out of the car, hurry to the passenger door, and open it for her, escorting her to the elevator. Once inside the condo, I toss my keys into the bowl by the door, and she kicks out of her shoes.

"Of course, you're not buying a house just because of me," she continues as we walk into the kitchen, and I reach for two glasses. One wine glass, and one whiskey glass.

I pour us each a drink and pass the wine to Annika.

"I mean, you have valid reasons for wanting a house *without* me."

"A?"

"Yes?"

"Stop talking." I clink my glass to hers, take a long sip of the whiskey, and then pull her in for a hug. "My mother spoke out of turn, that's all. I just have thoughts running through my head. But before I do anything that would commit either of us to something for the long haul, I'll have a conversation with you first. Okay?"

"Yeah. Okay. That sounds good."

She smiles up at me, looking relieved. I'm still stuck on her *for a little while* comment, but I decide to let it be for tonight.

We've made no promises.

But if she thinks I'll let her move away from me, she's got another think coming. But it's early days yet, and we're finally in a place of getting to know each other again—and being together.

The rest will happen in due time. For now, I'm going to enjoy the hell out of her.

At *her* pace.

"Are you sleepy?" I ask when I hear her yawn.

"I think the past week is catching up to me," she says and sips her wine as she follows me back to the bedroom. Of course, she's exhausted. She packed up her house, her business, and left her life in Denver. We wandered all over the market today, and she had dinner with my parents.

I'm surprised that she's still standing upright.

"I have an idea." I kiss her forehead, run my hands down her arms, and then lead her into the bathroom. "I think you need a hot bath."

"Oh, God, I've been *dying* to take a swim in that tub." She does a little happy dance. "You run the water, and I'll go get my things."

I take my time setting the temperature of the water, sprinkle in a generous amount of Epsom salts that smell like lavender, and light a few candles that I bought a day or two before Annika came to Seattle.

When she returns, her eyes widen.

"I might fall asleep."

"If you do, I'll wake you up. No drowning in my

tub." I tip up her chin so I can kiss her softly. "Just yell if you need anything."

"Thank you. This will be heaven."

I close the door behind me so she has privacy and find my laptop. I sit in the chair by the window and open the computer. I should check my email and see if any clients need me this week.

But things are quiet on the work front. It seems everyone is happy where they are for now. And I won't complain about that because it gives me more time with Annika.

I put the computer away and use the other bathroom to take a quick shower and change. When Annika's been in the bath for more than thirty minutes, I knock on the door, just to make sure she didn't make good on her word and fall asleep.

"You alive in there?"

"Oh, yeah. I'm just in bliss. But I'm a prune, so I'll be out soon."

"No hurry, honey. Just checking."

I turn down the bed and slip between the sheets, feeling exhausted myself, just as Annika steps out of the bathroom, a whoosh of warm air trailing after her.

"That was the best thing I've done in a *long* time," she announces as she tosses her dirty clothes into a hamper and then joins me in bed. "It might become a nightly ritual."

"Nothing wrong with that." I trail my fingertip

down her nose and then lean in to kiss her gently. I've been taking it slow with her. There's no need to hurry.

It's torture keeping my hands to myself. Keeping myself from stripping her bare and having my way with her.

But there's plenty of time for that.

Annika starts to unbutton her pajama shirt, but I take her hands and bring them to my mouth, then turn her away from me and press her back against my chest.

"Goodnight, sweetheart."

"'Night."

I'm just about to drop into sleep when I hear her sniffle. My eyes shoot open, and I frown as I pull Annika onto her back and cup her cheek gently.

"What's wrong?"

She shakes her head and tries to pull away, but I hold her close, panic setting up residence in my belly.

"Honey, I need you to tell me what I did wrong so I can fix it."

"I *am* too damaged," she says, her bottom lip quivering.

"What are you talking about?"

"You said that I wasn't, that everything I'd been through didn't repulse you. But, damn it, it's my second night here, and I just practically threw myself at you, and you turned me away."

She's crying in earnest now, and I feel like the biggest asshole to ever walk the face of the Earth.

"I didn't mean to turn you away." I wipe at her tears

and am pretty sure I'd like to beat myself up for causing them. "I just...I'm trying to take things slow."

"Why?"

"Because you *matter*, Annika. Because you've been through hell in the past year. And what kind of a prick would I be if I just jumped you? If I pushed you against the wall and had my way with you?"

"That sounds kind of fun."

I laugh in spite of myself and kiss her forehead. "We can put that on the schedule for a later date. I hate that today had awkward moments. Especially after we spent so many years together, and it was anything but awkward back then. But things have happened since then. Things that are absolutely *not* your fault. Not mine, either. We're getting to know each other again, in a way. I know who you are, and I can tell you that I'm as attracted to you today as I was the first time I saw you on campus."

"Really?" She sniffles, but her eyes are full of hope now. "I was afraid I'd made a mistake by coming here. That I'm intruding or something."

"No." I kiss her lips now. "Absolutely, not. I don't want the first time I take you to be when you're exhausted from wrapping up your previous life just *hours* before. Call me a romantic, but I want it to be more special than that. Because you deserve that and more, Annika."

"Wow, you *are* a romantic," she whispers. "Okay, that makes me feel a little better. But the next time I move to take my shirt off, don't humiliate me by patting me on the head and telling me to go to sleep."

"That's *not* what happened."

"Felt like it."

"Then I apologize for being a moron."

She laughs a little now. "Apology accepted. I *am* tired."

"Go to sleep." I kiss her once more. "Before I say fuck it to being romantic and make you *really* tired."

"Fine." She sighs and burrows face-first into my chest. "Goodnight, Rafe."

"Goodnight, Annika."

"I REALLY LOVE THIS KITCHEN," Annika says the next day as she starts to clean up from dinner. "That oven is just amazing. When did you have this place updated?"

"It was done about a year ago, I guess. Pop had the whole building updated. He went all out."

"You're not kidding."

"I can help with dishes."

"No." She holds up a hand. "Absolutely, not. You've made breakfast two days in a row, cleaned up, *and* helped me prep dinner. I've got this."

I'm relieved that she let me off of the hook for KP duty because I have a little surprise for her. So, I nod solemnly and promise to be back shortly.

I walk to the bedroom and set my plan in motion. I

have rose petals to spread over the floor, the tub, the bed. I have roses in vases. I have candles to light.

In less than thirty minutes, the bedroom is transformed into a romantic suite, complete with champagne.

I'm going to romance my girl.

When I return to the kitchen, Annika is just putting away the last of the dishes, humming to herself.

"How do you feel?" I ask.

"Pretty good, actually. Not too full, not too tired."

"Excellent. Come with me. I want to show you something."

She grins and takes my hand. "Okay. What do you have to show me?"

"You'll see."

With her hand linked to mine, I lead her down the hallway and open the bedroom door.

"Your suite awaits."

Her eyes grow wide as she steps inside, and then she turns to me. "How in the hell did you pull all of this off? We were together most of the day."

"You took a nap," I reply easily. "I ran an errand or two."

"No kidding." She sighs and brushes her fingertips over a rose, then buries her nose in the fragrant bloom. "This is so lovely."

"Not nearly as lovely as you."

I wrap my arms around her from behind and kiss the shell of her ear.

"Do you mind if I take a bath?" she asks, and I just smile and open the bathroom door, where I have more candles lit, a full, steaming tub with more rose petals floating on the water. "Holy cow."

"I want you to relax. I want you to feel pampered and appreciated."

"Mission accomplished." She tests the water with her fingers. "I promise not to drown."

"Good idea. Because I have plans for you when you get out of this tub."

Her eyes shine with mischief and lust when they find mine. "Promise?"

"Hell, yes."

"Then let me get in the water." She shoos me out of the room, closes the door, and I take a long breath.

She likes it.

Hopefully, she likes everything else that's about to come, as well. I'm going to take my time. I'm going to relearn and examine every inch of her perfect little body.

Similar to the night before, I go down the hall to the guest bathroom. I already stocked it with my shaving supplies, so I do that first. Then I take a shower and pull on only a simple pair of black boxer shorts.

If all goes according to plan, they won't be on for long.

I've just walked back into the bedroom when the bathroom door opens, and standing as a silhouette against the light of the bathroom behind her, Annika pauses and bites her lip. She's the most beautiful woman I've ever seen in my life.

I mean, I already knew that, but with her standing there in a sexy black nighty that I didn't even see her grab earlier, my heart simply stalls in my chest. My mouth goes dry. My dick comes to attention.

"I want to fuck you in that doorway." My voice is pure gravel. The pulse in Annika's throat jumps. "But I'm not going to. Not right now."

"It's on the schedule for later with the against-the-wall sex?" she asks, her voice breathless.

"Oh, yeah. It's on the damn schedule. I want you with an ache that never really goes away, Annika." I'm slowly stalking toward her as I talk. I'm afraid to reach out for her because I know I won't stop once I touch her. "I tried for years to extinguish that desire. To tell myself that I'd never have you. That you couldn't be mine.

"But there was always something inside me, a voice or an ache, that wouldn't shut up. That wouldn't *give* up. You kept telling me no, but I knew that I'd have you with me again someday. I didn't know when or how, but I knew in the deepest part of me that you'd make your way back to me."

I swallow hard and reach out to touch just the very edge of her earlobe.

She shivers.

"Everything about you is a miracle." I step closer.

"And I want you to not only *hear* that but also believe it. Because it's true. You're my miracle, Annika."

"Rafe?"

I just look her in the eyes.

"I'm going to need you to touch me now."

CHAPTER 11

~ANNIKA~

*I*s someone hammering the wall next to me? Or is that just my heart, thundering in my chest?

The way Rafe's looking at me would make any woman melt into a puddle. His eyes, so brilliantly blue, are on *fire*. Intently watching me as he slowly walks closer as if he's a big cat, stalking his prey.

And let me just say, I'm more than happy to be the prey. I'll gladly sign up for that mission.

I volunteer as tribute.

"My knees are shaky," I say, surprised to hear the shake in my voice.

"Let's help you out with that."

He scoops me into his strong arms and carries me to the bed, where he lays me on the sheets covered in rose petals.

I didn't expect Rafe to go all out like this. He didn't

even do this when I lost my virginity to him. But it's so incredibly sweet, and so thoughtful.

So *Rafe*.

"I don't know where you bought this thing," he says as he pushes a finger under the black strap on my shoulder and runs it up and down. "But we're only shopping there from now on."

I grin and reach up to brush my fingers through his damp hair. "Like that, do you?"

"Yeah. Yeah, I like it. It's going to look fucking awesome on my floor."

I snort, all awkwardness gone between us. And when that finger glides down my chest and brushes over the tip of my breast, I sigh.

"You were hot at nineteen," he murmurs and gets to work unfastening the little black number I wear. "I couldn't keep my hands off of you. I could *wait* for you to be ready for a moment like this."

"I made you wait for a long time."

"It was worth it." He swallows hard when he uncovers my breasts, then licks his lips. "A man should have to earn this, A. And I just have to say, if you were hot then, and you *were*, you're beyond my wildest dreams now."

"Rafe—"

"It's true." His eyes fly to mine and glow in the light from the bathroom. "Jesus. Your body matured into a gorgeous work of art."

"Yeah, I'm not as skinny anymore. I have hips and boobs, and—"

"Curves," he interrupts. "They're called curves, baby. And if you say anything bad about them, I might have to take you over my knee."

"Well, that would be horrible." My dry, sarcastic comment makes him chuckle as he kisses his way down my torso. "You're just so good with your mouth."

"I'm glad you think so. Because it's going to be *all over* you."

"That sounds like a threat."

"Promise." He kisses the tender flesh just above my navel, hooks his fingers into the thin straps on the poor excuse for panties I'm wearing, and guides them down my legs before tossing them on the floor. "It's a promise. I hope you don't have plans tonight because this will take a while."

"And here I was hoping to run out and catch a late show." I grin, but then sigh when Rafe parts my legs and places a kiss on my inner thigh, about six inches below the promised land.

How often did I dream of exactly this? Long for it? Even after I moved to Denver and met the jerk that became my husband, I thought of Rafe. No matter how hard I tried to block him from my mind, it was no use.

Because being with him feels right. I belong here in his arms. In his bed.

I gasp when he blows gently on my core, and when

he dips his head to brush his tongue over my hard clit, I have to grab onto the sheets to anchor myself.

"Hold onto me," he instructs. I follow his orders and plunge my fingers into his hair. When his mouth returns to me, my hands clench, hard.

My God.

My toes curl. My stomach and butt clench, making me rise off the mattress, and Rafe uses the opportunity to slip his hands under me. He cups my ass and holds me so he can feast at his leisure.

He changes rhythms, moving from quick, pulsing motions to long, leisurely licks. My body is on a roller coaster of sensation, and it just might kill me.

But what a way to go.

When he slips two fingers inside me, I come apart at the seams. I can't see or hear. I can't do *anything* except ride wave after wave of sensation.

And when my brain starts to clear, I feel Rafe move, shift his body to between my legs, and settle in over me, his elbows planted on either side of my head.

"Amazing," he whispers.

"Yeah, it was."

My eyes flutter open to find him smiling softly down at me. With those blue eyes tied to mine, he slips gently inside of me and stops to let me adjust—the way he always did before.

Rafe is blessed in the penis department. But it doesn't take long for my body to loosen. When it does, he moves in long, fluid thrusts. His pubis rubs against my clit with each stroke, and I know without a shadow of a doubt that I'm about to fall over the cliff into bliss again at any moment.

"Rafe."

"Yes, baby?" He kisses the side of my mouth, then takes one hand and pins it above my head. "I'm right here."

"Oh, God."

With three more thrusts, I succumb to the orgasm, shivering and clenching around him. With a muttered curse, Rafe follows me over.

We're panting and clinging to each other. It's been *so long,* and yet it feels like no time has passed at all.

"That was a good start."

His head comes up, and he stares down at me before letting out a loud laugh.

"A good *start?*"

"Hmm." I stretch lazily when he rolls away. I'm about to get off the bed to go clean up when Rafe walks into the bathroom. I hear the water running. When he returns, he wipes me with a warm washcloth. "Oh, that's nice."

He grins, tosses the rag into the laundry basket, and then curls up next to me.

"Rafe?"

"Yes, babe." He kisses my temple.

"I want something sweet."

He boosts up on his elbow and brushes a strand of hair off my cheek. "What kind of something sweet?"

"Cheesecake."

He cocks a brow. "We don't have any cheesecake."

"I think I saw a diner down the street. They probably have cheesecake."

"So, we're going out then?"

"Yes." I jump up from the bed, feeling newly energized. Some muscles will be sore in the morning, but deliciously so. "I'm just going to slip into some clothes."

"The more you put on, the more I have to take off later."

"You're a big, strong man. You can handle it."

"How many blue shirts does one person need?" Rafe demands as he holds out a navy-blue blouse for me to put on a hanger and add to the closet.

Since I'm officially staying in the master bedroom, Rafe offered the *gorgeous* closet to me since what he has doesn't fill even a fraction of it.

I didn't say no.

"There are many different shades of blue," I inform him and take the blouse from him. "This is navy, but that next one is cerulean."

"Cer-what?"

"Cerulean. And then you have your baby blue, cobalt, indigo, teal—"

"Okay, okay." He laughs and passes me another top.

"I get it. You need a lot of blue. And every other color, it seems."

"I like clothes." I shrug and open another new container of hangers. "Just wait until we find the box full of pretty party dresses. Those are my favorite. I don't go to many parties or formal events, but a girl needs to have plenty of options on hand, just in case."

"I can't wait."

I glance at him and grin. "You know, you don't have to help me in here. I can manage all of this. I'm sure you have stuff to do."

"I don't mind." His phone rings, just as mine does at the same time. "Shane."

"Ivie."

"Put us on speaker," Ivie says as soon as I answer. Rafe already has Shane on speaker when I get Ivie set up, and then they both announce, "We're getting married!"

"Uh, we know. Shane proposed weeks ago," I reply.

"No, we're getting married *now*," Ivie says. "Well, soon anyway. We're on our way to Seattle right now."

"We haven't finished with the plans," I reply, starting to panic. "A lot goes into a wedding, Ivie."

"That's just it," Shane adds. "We don't really want a big wedding."

"So, we're going to Vegas!" Ivie squeals. "All of us. Get packed because we're leaving tonight."

"Who else is going?" I ask.

"Curt's with us, much to his dismay," Ivie says. Curt

is one of Shane's closest friends and the manager of Shane's ranch in Colorado. "Nadia and Carmine are flying into Vegas tomorrow morning."

"But they're on their honeymoon."

"They're headed back this way, on their way to some posh spot in Europe. They're going to make a stop in Vegas to celebrate with us."

"Did you invite the parents?" Rafe asks his brother.

"We talked to Mom and Pop," Shane says. "They're fine with this, as long as we let Mom throw us a big reception at some point."

Ivie's parents are dead, but my family thinks of her as ours.

"Even Uncle Igor was happy with it," Ivie adds. "It's all set. Seriously, pack. Oh my gosh, it's going to be *so fun.*"

They both hang up, and Rafe and I just stare at each other in surprise and then bust up laughing.

"So, I guess we're going to Vegas."

"Never a dull moment with this family," he says, shaking his head and tapping on his phone.

"I'll finish unpacking a few boxes, and then I'll pack. They won't be here for a while yet."

I pull the tape on a box, open the flaps, and hear Rafe mutter, "Good God."

"What?"

"Is that all *white* shirts?"

"Yeah." I look down with a frown. "I mean, you need white shirts, Rafe."

"How many? There's only one shade of white, A."

I cross my arms over my chest, knowing that it boosts my boobs and he can see plenty of cleavage. "I don't know." I tap my lips as if I'm giving it a lot of thought. "There's cream, eggshell, pearl, alabaster—"

He moves quickly, way faster than you'd expect for a man Rafe's size, and crushes me to him, pressing his lips to mine and making me forget how to breathe right.

"That shut you up," he says against my lips.

"I don't remember what we were talking about."

He laughs, pats me on the butt, and looks ridiculously proud of himself when I have to sit on the ottoman to get my bearings. But then the box at my feet reminds me.

"I really need to get this done. I can't pack if I don't know where all of my clothes are."

"Of course, not. If you have this under control, I'll go pack some things and make sure the jet will be ready."

"I've totally got it under control." I wave him off and reach for a cream blouse to hang.

"Do you want anything? A latte?"

"Oh my God, I'd give my right ovary for a latte."

"No need for that." Rafe leans in to kiss me. "I'll bring you one in a bit."

"You're handy to have around." I blow him a kiss and reach for another hanger. "I need to call Ivie back. I don't even know what she wants me to wear."

"Shit, you're right. I'd better ask Shane if he wants me to bring a suit. I'll see you in a bit."

"Okay." I reach for my phone as Rafe leaves and dial Ivie's number. I grin at the happiness in her voice when she answers.

"Hey there, bestie."

"You sound ecstatic."

"Are you kidding? I'm getting married in *Vegas*. How cool is that?"

"Very cool." Not what I would pick, but I'm thrilled that she's getting what she wants. "I need to know what the dress code is. Do I get to wear something fancy?"

"Hell, yes. I bought a gorgeous white dress that isn't technically a wedding dress, but it's going to be awesome. I know you have a closet full of nice dresses. Pick one."

"Is there a particular color you want me to wear?"

"You're beautiful in anything. Seriously, you choose."

"I'm going to bring a couple of choices, and we can decide together."

"Good idea. We're in the car headed to the airfield now. We'll be in Seattle by early afternoon. If all goes well, the five of us will be on the jet by dinnertime."

"Sounds good to me. And because I *am* your best friend, and I love you, I'm just going to double-check. This is what you want, right? You're not just doing this because you don't want to ask my uncle to pay for a big wedding?"

"No. Honest. Shane and I were talking about it, and we both think it sounds like fun. Spontaneous."

"It is that," I agree. "Okay, you sound excited, so I am, too. I'll be ready when you get here."

"Annika, I'm so happy. Like, *so happy.* I didn't think this could ever happen to me, and then Shane just burst into my life and wouldn't take no for an answer."

"The Martinelli men all have that in common." I finish hanging up the last of the *white* shirts and turn to open another box. "They're charming, and persistent."

"And don't forget sexy," Ivie reminds me. "Okay, we'll talk more when we have Nadia with us. I can't wait to hear about her honeymoon."

"Me, too. I hope they're having fun."

"Are you and Rafe doing okay?" she asks.

"Things were a little awkward at first, but they are calming down. We're growing more comfortable with each other. And now that sex is involved—"

"*Sex* is involved?" she interrupts. "Oh, man, I can't wait to hear about this. And I'll want all the details. Shane, hurry. I need to get to Annika."

"I'm going as fast as I'm allowed under the penalty of law," I hear him reply.

"Go faster," she replies. "Okay, I'll see you in a few hours."

"See you soon."

I hang up and dig in, truly wanting to be settled into this closet.

A couple of hours later, with an empty latte cup on

the ottoman, all of my things are on hangers or tucked into drawers. My bags are on shelves. Shoes organized.

It's glorious.

And now, I have to pack to go see my best friend marry the love of her life.

CHAPTER 12

~ANNIKA~

"Carmine and Nadia just arrived," Rafe says as he walks into our hotel suite and sits on the bed next to me, where I'm nursing a hangover. Ivie and I had one too many celebratory shots of tequila last night.

Or seven too many.

But the drunk sex when Rafe and I got back to the room was *so* worth it.

"I brought you coffee," Rafe adds.

"Oh, thank God." I take the mug from him and take a long, grateful sip. "My God, I drank too much last night. And the worst part is, we'll probably do it all again tonight."

"You don't *have* to drink," he reminds me and pushes my hair over my shoulder. "You can pass."

"Yeah, I might do that. We'll see how things shake

out. Now, I have to get myself together so I can hurry up to Ivie's suite and help her get ready."

"I'm meeting with the guys here in a little while. We're going to get ready in Carmine's room and when we're all good to go, we'll meet up with you ladies in the lobby."

"That sounds good." I take a deep breath, another sip of coffee, and lean over to rest my head on Rafe's shoulder. "I'm glad we came. It's a fun distraction."

"Did you need to be distracted?"

"No, but it's a good one all the same." I sigh. "Okay, I need to hop in the shower and get over there."

"I'd join you, but I'm worried that Shane will eat all the bacon." He kisses me on the nose, then pulls me off the bed. "Have fun. Call me if you need me."

"Same goes." I wave as Rafe heads for the door, grabbing his bag on the way out. When the door closes behind him, I take another deep breath.

I'm in Vegas, with all of the people I love the most, and I'm *with* Rafe. For the first time ever, I don't have to pretend that I don't love him. Everyone knows that we're together.

The shower helps to rejuvenate me, and by the time I wrap myself in a robe, pile my wet hair in a knot on top of my head, and gather all of my supplies to head over to Ivie's room, I almost feel like myself again. Which is good because Ivie's getting married, and I want to feel my best.

I make sure I have my room key in my bag and then

head down the hall to Ivie's room. We're all staying at the Wynn, and we've taken over a floor of suites.

Because, of course, we have.

We're two wealthy families, which means that while Ivie may be eloping, it'll still be done in style.

I don't have to knock on the door because Shane's coming out of the room as I arrive.

"Hey," he says with a grin. "The other two are waiting for you."

"Thanks. How are you holding up?"

"I'm fantastic. The day can't go fast enough for me."

He holds the door for me, then waves at Ivie, who's just seen me, and claps her hands in excitement.

"See you soon, babe," he says and lets the door close behind me.

"He's about to be my *husband*," Ivie says before throwing her arms around me in a big hug. "How do you feel?"

"Hungover. Why aren't you in pain?"

"I was for a few minutes but then I took a shower. Now, I'm fine. Nadia just ordered all the food in the world, and we have hair and makeup people coming in about an hour."

"Whoa." I stop cold and stare at my cousin after rounding the corner to the dining room. She's tanned and looks damn happy with herself. "You're gorgeous. Obviously, the honeymoon agrees with you."

"I'd like to be on a honeymoon all the time," Nadia replies as she stands and wraps her arms around me.

"It's going well. And this was a fun surprise to throw into the mix."

"Food's here!" Ivie announces at the sound of the doorbell.

"She's so *happy*," Nadia whispers to me. "She's giddy. I've never seen her like this. Ever."

"I know, and I like it. She's excited to marry him. He makes her happy."

"Clearly." Nadia turns her shrewd eyes to me. "When's it your turn?"

"He hasn't asked me. Besides, it's too soon."

"He'll ask," she says simply as a man rolls a big table full of food into the room. "You can leave that there. We'll take over."

After he collects his tip and leaves, we each pile plates full of food and sit at the table.

"So, you're getting hitched." Nadia shoves some melon into her mouth. "I want to see the dress."

"After I eat. I don't want to mess it up," Ivie replies. "Tell us about your honeymoon. Where have you been again?"

"Bora Bora," she says. "Let's just say it's been nothing but sex, lying in the sun, eating all the food, and more sex."

"God, that sounds horrible." I shake my head, feeling only a little jealous. "Your skin is glowing. Is that from all the sun, or all the sex?"

"Both." Nadia eats a strawberry and turns to Ivie. "Are you and Shane taking a honeymoon?"

"Not right away. I don't know where I want to go. He said we can go literally *anywhere*, and that overwhelmed me, so I'm thinking about it."

"There's a resort in Bora Bora I can recommend," Nadia says with a wink. "Do we have time to go shopping? Or should we wait until after the wedding?"

"Depends on what we're shopping for," I reply. "Actually, strike that. No, we don't have time. When Nadia shops, it's an Olympic event. We'd better save that for tomorrow."

"I never got Carmine a wedding gift," she says. "And it's been bothering me. He not only got me this ridiculous rock but he also bought me a *new car.* Like, a whole car. A Porsche. I mean, who does that?"

"The Martinellis," Ivie and I say in unison, making us laugh.

"What are you going to get him?" I ask her.

"There's a special Rolex that I want to get him. And it's rare. But I made some calls on the down-low, and a boutique here has one in stock. They're holding it for me."

"Carmine likes watches, doesn't he?" I ask.

"Yeah. It's like me and handbags," Nadia replies with a shrug. "He'll die when he opens it. So, we'll go fetch it tomorrow morning. What did you get Shane, Ivie?"

Ivie blushes and then shrugs. "Nothing yet."

"But you have a plan." I lean forward. "Spill it."

"We're going to try to get pregnant," she says. "I

want babies, you guys. And he does, too. So, we're working on it."

I blink at her. "Your wedding gift to Shane is the possibility of children?"

Ivie frowns. "Well, yeah. I guess. Damn it, is that lame?"

"Kinda lame," Nadia says. "We can do better than that."

"I don't think he needs a watch," Ivie says, thinking it over. "And he has all the electronic gadgets anyone needs. He doesn't wear jewelry. He's not fancy. Dear God, what do I get him?"

"Okay, don't panic," I say and reach over to put my hand on hers. "Obviously, there's no huge rush here. Just think it over and get him something *sometime*."

"Yeah, okay." Ivie takes a breath. "I'm going to show you guys my dress before the hair and makeup girls get here. Come on."

We file into the suite's second bedroom and watch as Ivie unzips a long garment bag, then peels it back.

"Holy shit." Nadia walks closer. "It sparkles."

"This is gorgeous, Ivie."

The dress is white and covered in gorgeous crystals that sparkle in the light. It's form-fitting and looks like the hem will hit just below the knee.

The bodice has a sweetheart neckline, and it's strapless.

"You'll be a bombshell in this," I inform my friend.

"Shane will pass right out, and the boys will have to pick him up."

"I hope so," Ivie replies just as the doorbell rings again. "Okay, let's get this show on the road."

IVIE IS *gorgeous* in her dress, with her hair loose and curly, and her makeup done absolutely perfectly.

Nadia chose a red cocktail dress with a lace neckline, and I'm in a purple number that I've been *dying* to wear somewhere.

All of the guys are in suits.

Shane sprung for the best elopement package, complete with a photographer, flowers, and music.

And I have to admit, it's really beautiful.

"You married me." Ivie cuddles up to Shane in the limo, her bouquet still clutched in her hand.

"And I'd do it again," Shane says, kissing her on the forehead.

"Rafe and I put our heads together," Carmine says, catching all of our attention. "And rather than go out to eat with a bunch of strangers in a restaurant, we brought the party to us. We'll be in a private dining room at the hotel."

"That's so nice," Ivie says just as the limo stops at the hotel entrance where someone is waiting to usher us into a private elevator and up to the private suite for our makeshift reception.

The room is beautiful, with candlelight, a cake, and a table set with gorgeous flatware and more flowers.

"This was a good idea," I whisper to Rafe. "More intimate and special."

"That was the goal." He presses his hand to the small of my back. "Have I mentioned that you're stunning in this dress?"

"About a dozen times."

"Here's lucky number thirteen. You're a vision, Annika."

"Well, thank you very much. And you look dapper in this suit." I run a finger down his lapel.

"I hate wearing suits."

"I thought all mafiosos wore suits every day."

He smirks and shakes his head. "Hell, no. Only in the movies. Or if you're my dad."

"I'd like to propose a toast," Carmine says, raising his glass and catching our attention. "And maybe give a little speech. Bear with me. I'm happy for the both of you, Shane and Ivie. That you endured everything that happened a couple of months ago together and came out on the other side stronger. You clearly love each other very much and are happy together. So, here's to a lifetime of love and laughter. No matter what might come up, if you hang onto each other, you'll be okay. To Ivie and Shane."

"To Ivie and Shane," we agree and drink our champagne.

Dinner is a delicious steak with salad and potatoes

and fresh asparagus. There's more food than most of us can eat.

And when it comes time to cut the cake, Ivie only gets a little frosting up Shane's nose.

But Shane gently holds the fork for her, not getting a speck on her.

"Well, that's no fun," Rafe mutters, making me laugh.

"It's respectful," I say, nudging him with my hip.

"How long do we have to stay?" Rafe asks, and I frown up at him.

"What do you mean? This is *your brother's* wedding, Rafe. We stay until it's over."

He sighs as if he's suffering.

"Why do you want to go?"

"I haven't had my hands on you in almost twenty-four hours."

His blue eyes shine as he stares down at me.

"I'm going to the bathroom. Meet me there."

Without waiting for him to reply, I walk away, through a small bedroom, and into the adjoining bath.

He doesn't knock.

He just walks right through the door, locks it behind him, and comes for me, his mouth set in firm lines. He's all business as he turns me away from him so I'm facing the mirror. He watches me in the reflection.

"This isn't going to be soft and gentle," he warns me.

"Fine by me." I shimmy my skirt up around my hips

as he fumbles with his pants. The next thing I know, he bends me over and slides right inside.

"Jesus, you're so fucking wet."

"Always when you're around." I grab onto the edge of the vanity. "Oh, God, yes. Oh. This is a good angle."

"Fucking hell." His voice is a primal growl. He grips my hips, his fingers almost biting into my flesh as he fucks me hard from behind. I can't help the small cry that rips from my throat when I come, and then the whimper when he follows me over.

This might be the fastest quickie we've ever had.

But it was damn good.

And when he slips out of me and wipes off before tucking himself away, he looks mighty proud of himself.

"See?" I say as I wiggle my skirt back down into place. "Now we don't have to leave the party. But I do have to clean up, thanks to gravity. You go out first. I'll follow you."

He frames my face in his hands and kisses me long and slow. Finally, with a smile, he leaves the bathroom, and I take a moment to catch my breath and clean up.

That was unexpected.

When I walk back into the party, I'm met with sober faces and silence.

"What's wrong?" I ask immediately and hurry to Rafe. "What's happened?"

"We just got a call from Pop," he replies grimly.

"Another boss and his family are dead. The Giovannis in Kansas City."

"This is a pattern," Nadia says. "Three families, all assassinated. These aren't unrelated. Someone is picking off syndicate families, one by one."

"Agreed," Carmine says and turns to Shane. "And I'm sorry that this call came in today."

"It pisses me off that it's happening at all," Shane replies. I wish I had my equipment, but I do have a computer in my room."

"I do, too," Ivie says. "We can do some digging tonight. Are the parents safe?"

"Igor said they're fine for now," Carmine says. "And I'll call Pop. I think we should have Igor and Katya come to Seattle where we can have them in one spot with Mom and Pop. Keep them all safe while we figure this out."

"My father has an army," Nadia reminds her husband. "He is capable of keeping himself and Mom safe."

"He can bring his army with him," Carmine says. "They're safer together, and we all know it."

"Let's take the cake back to our suite," Ivie suggests. "We can work and nibble on this there."

"You shouldn't have to work on your wedding night," I say, but Ivie just shakes her head.

"It's fine. Really. I had the best day ever, and now I get to do some hacking while eating delicious cake.

Life's good. Let's go find the bastards behind this and make them pay."

"You've become a total mafioso wife," I accuse her with a laugh.

"Yeah, thanks." She wipes an imaginary tear from the corner of her eye. "It makes me all sentimental."

CHAPTER 13

~RAFE~

"*N*ow that everyone's under one roof, security is in place, and we feel generally safe right now, let's go down and work out," Carmine suggests. We returned to Seattle from Vegas two days ago. We got our parents and the Tarenkovs settled into our grandmother's estate yesterday.

An army of men patrols the grounds at all times.

No one will get through.

And I could use some time in the gym with a punching bag.

"I'm down," Shane says. "Let's all meet down there in twenty? I could take a round with Rocco in the ring."

"If you plan on dying today," I say with a grin. "Yeah, we'll meet you down there."

I hurry up the stairs to the room that Annika used during Carmine and Nadia's wedding. This time, I'm not next to her. I'm staying *with* her. Just as it should be.

"Hey," Annika says when I walk through the door. "I was wondering where you ran off to."

"I was chatting with the brothers. Are you in the mood to work out?"

She arches a brow. "Sure. Where?"

"Just get dressed, and I'll show you."

"Okay, mysterious man." She jumps up and changes into leggings and a sports bra, then turns to me. "I'm ready."

"Not like that, you aren't."

She scowls and looks down at herself. "What's wrong with this?"

"It's a *bra.* You need a shirt over it."

"It's a sports bra. This can be the shirt."

"No."

She sets her hands on her hips and glares at me. "A bathing suit covers more. You're being a caveman. Let's go work out."

I cross my arms over my chest and stand firm. "If you think I'll let my brothers see you in that getup—"

"You're ridiculous." She flings her hands into the air and stomps to the dresser where she pulls out a tank and slips it over her head. "There, master. I'm all covered up. Happy?"

I grin. "Yes, actually."

"You know, you don't get to dictate everything I wear."

Before I can open the door of our room, I turn and pin her against the wall, my face inches from hers as I nibble her bottom lip. "Your outfit is sexy as fuck. I know my brothers love their girls, but they'd *see* that, and I don't want to have to kill them today. It's a simple tank top, A."

"Does this mean I can't wear a bikini when I go to the pool?"

"No." But the thought doesn't sit well with me. "I suppose not."

She laughs and pushes at my shoulder. "You're cute when you pout."

"I'm not pouting."

"Right. Not at all. Come on, let's work out. I didn't know there was a gym in this place."

"It's in the basement." I lead her to the elevator and refrain from pinning her against the wall, right here and now.

When we get to the basement entrance, the other four are already there, along with Curt, who's also riding this thing out here at Gram's house. Carmine is keying in the code to the heavy, iron door.

"What the hell is this place?" Nadia demands as the door swings open. "And why didn't you tell us about it before?"

"We were busy," Shane says with a shrug. "Okay, we have the gym over there. Through that door is the artillery vault and firing range."

"Holy shit," Ivie whispers. "It's a mini version of the ranch."

Shane turns and kisses her on the mouth. "Now you're just flattering me."

"This is crazy," Nadia breathes. "I want to see the weapons before we work out."

"Okay." Carmine presses his palm to the plate next to the door. When it opens, we all file in, and the lights automatically come on. The glass cases are also well lit, displaying all different kinds of weapons from daggers to automatic weapons.

Annika pulls her hand from mine and lifts a 9mm pistol out of the case.

"Whoa." I reach out and take the gun from her. "I don't think you should be handling this."

"Is it loaded?"

"They're all loaded, sweetheart. These are all dangerous weapons. A novice shouldn't be playing with them."

She nods, stares at the gun in my hand, and then takes it back. "Where's the firing range?"

Nadia snorts, but I don't look her way. "Over there."

"Let's go." She leads the way to one of the firing lanes, sets up a target, and sends it down the line. Then, without missing a beat, she pops the magazine out of the gun, examines it, pops it back in, loads one in the chamber, and lifts both hands. She fires a single round, pulls the magazine out of the weapon before setting it down, and pushes the button to fetch the target.

We're all quiet, watching intently.

And when the target arrives, there's a single hole in the forehead of the outline of a man.

I blink at her and then the target again.

"Nadia taught me," is all Annika says.

"Did you think I'd let the niece of a boss go through life unable to protect herself?" Nadia demands, still grinning. "Annika is a hell of a shot. And she knows her way around any weapon you have in there. She's no pussy."

I'm so turned on right now, I can hardly breathe.

"Do you have any more *mansplaining* you'd like to do?" Annika asks.

My brothers crack up.

Ivie and Nadia both high-five her.

Without saying a word, I pick her up and toss her over my shoulder.

"Hey!" Annika says and smacks me on the ass.

"I think Annika's about to get lucky," I hear Ivie say.

"Dude, you're a caveman," Shane calls out, and I throw up my hand, flipping them all the bird as they laugh and jeer behind us.

I don't break my stride as I choose the stairs rather than the elevator. I'm barely breathing hard when I reach our room.

Once inside, I put her on her feet and stare into mutinous blue eyes.

"That was *embarrassing*."

"Why?" I trap her against the wall the way I did not

long ago before we went downstairs. "Because I hauled you out of there?"

"Over your *shoulder*."

"Damn right. It was that or drag you, and carrying you was easier."

Her eyes narrow. "What's wrong with you?"

"I'm so turned on, I can't see straight."

That stops her. Her mouth opens and closes until she settles on, "What?"

"You heard me." I nip the side of her mouth. "I had no idea you could shoot like that. It was a lightning bolt straight through me. Jesus, seeing you hold a gun like that was the sexiest thing I've ever seen. I needed you. I *need* you. And you said you wanted to have sex pushed up against the wall."

"So that's moved up on the schedule, then?"

I grin and tear her leggings at the crotch. "Hell, yes."

There are no more words as we rip our clothes from our bodies. When I sink inside her, it's like coming home. I'm an animal. I can't go slow; I can't take my time.

All I can think about is the overwhelming drive to *mate* with her.

And when she moans with that gritty, dirty edge to her voice and clamps around my cock, it's my undoing. I empty myself inside her and have to lean on the wall to catch my breath.

"Well." Annika swallows hard. "That was fun. Let's put it back on the schedule for another time."

I laugh and set her on her feet. "I always have time for this."

"I WANT to go over everything we know," Pop says later in the evening when we're all together with our drinks of choice. Pop sits next to Igor, while Mom and Katya are seated by the window, drinking wine.

Curt, Shane, Carmine, and I are seated at a table with a glass of whiskey, and the girls are on couches, lounging with their wine and eating chocolate ice cream from the tub.

It's as casual as it gets around here, and my grandmother would have loved it.

"We have three bosses and their families, all murdered, in the last few weeks," Igor says, rubbing his chin. "Not by the same methods. No notes left behind, and no family taking credit for it."

"There was a car accident," Carmine adds, picking up the facts. "Killed the boss, his wife, and their daughter in Chicago. Then, we have the family in Boston, who were all sent into the water with cement shoes."

"This last one in Kansas City is even more disturbing," Pop says, shaking his head. "The boss and his wife had their throats slashed. The children, both under the age of twelve, were drugged and left for dead. One child, the youngest son, survived and is in the hospital under constant supervision."

"Has anyone called Elena?" Mom asks, catching our attention.

"Shit, I'll do that as soon as we're done here," Carmine says. "She and Archer are in Oregon, tucked away."

"Why do you need to call your cousin?" Nadia asks, frowning. "She's been on the down-low for years."

"We'll send some extra men to keep an eye on her," Carmine replies. "Besides, after what happened to her parents, we've always been more careful where she's concerned."

"What happened to her parents again? I know someone killed them, but I don't know the story."

"My sister, Claudia, was married to Vinnie Watkins, who was the boss at the time. Vinnie was a piece of shit, but he was still the boss," Pop says, telling the story. "When Elena was about twenty, I guess, Vinnie went to prison. He got too cocky with some money laundering and got caught. It was disgraceful. He was too prideful. While in prison, someone killed him."

"Claudia was killed in a car accident," Mom says, picking up the story, "on the same day."

"It wasn't an accident," Pop insists, slamming his fist on the table. "She was murdered."

"Well, we weren't able to prove that, were we?" Mom asks. "Carlo's mother, the woman who owned this house, spent many years trying to find those responsible for her daughter's death. Also, within hours of Claudia and Vinnie being killed, she hid Elena away. From all of us. For over a decade, we all thought Elena was also dead, her body not likely to be found."

"They didn't tell you that they were hiding Elena away?" Annika asks, shocked.

"No," Pop says. "However, *I* knew. I was the only one who did. Because the men my mother hired to help Elena disappear worked for *me*. Not her. I didn't tell anyone else because they didn't need to know. The fewer who knew, the safer Elena was."

"Still not happy that you didn't tell us," Carmine says, but Pop just shrugs.

"I run my house the way I see fit, and you know that. I don't apologize for it. Elena was safer because she was gone."

"I'm calling her now," Carmine says, tapping his phone. After three rings, Elena answers.

"Hey, favorite cousin," she says.

"I heard that," I call out.

"You're all my favorite, Rocco," she reminds me and makes me smile. "What's up with you guys?"

"Are you and Archer still in Oregon?" Carmine asks.

"Yeah, we're at the beach house. It's been a nice break, but I think we're heading back to the city in a couple of days."

"I want you to stay where you are," Pop says sternly. "Some things are happening here that I don't want you around for. Stay there with your husband. I'll have some men come to keep an eye on things, as well."

"Something big is going down," Elena says, her voice sober. "Don't worry, we'll cooperate. I'm happy to spend more time at the beach."

"Good girl," Pop says. "We'll be in touch."

"I'll call you soon," Carmine adds and clicks off.

"So, the people who killed Elena's parents are killing the other bosses?" Annika says.

We all look her way and frown.

"Not necessarily," Pop says. "What happened to Claudia and Vinnie was more than a decade ago. This isn't related."

"I don't think you're seeing the big picture," Annika disagrees. "And I don't mean that to sound disrespectful. Let's outline this. Bosses and their entire immediate families are coming up dead—all murdered in different ways. Your sister and brother-in-law were murdered. And your mother feared for Elena's life so much that she sent her away. She thought it was even a secret, so she could keep her safe. Why would she think that Elena would be killed? Most of the time, when a boss is murdered, the rest of their family isn't executed, as well."

"But why would they wait so long to continue?" Shane asks.

"Everyone is always saying that the mafia has a long memory," Nadia points out. "And they're not wrong. This started all those years ago with Elena's parents.

And now, someone is systematically making their way through all of the prominent families in the country."

"We're going to find them," I promise. "And we're going to end them."

"Oh, we certainly are," Nadia agrees. "But we need to know where to start."

"Gram has boxes and boxes full of research," Shane says, thinking it over. "When we discovered that Elena was alive and were trying to find her, we found the boxes. She must have hired dozens of investigators to find the killer or killers and filed everything away methodically. There has to be something in there that she missed."

"Well, we have a whole room full of fresh eyes," Ivie says. "And I don't mean to sound heartless, but some of us aren't personally connected. Maybe we'll see something that your grandmother didn't."

"You're forgetting something," Igor says, speaking for the first time as he turns to Pop. "We're in *your* home, my friend. Anything here, including the investigative reports, are proprietary to your family. If you don't want my family digging into that business, I understand."

All eyes turn to Pop, who's rubbing his chin again.

"If I didn't trust you and the rest of your family, Igor, you wouldn't be in my family's home. You know that. This doesn't just impact my family now. It affects yours, as well as all of the other organizations in the country. Perhaps the world. If something here can help solve this mystery, it's open to all of you. Your firefly is right. Fresh eyes are helpful. Our young people are intelligent. And we're stronger together."

Igor nods, happy with Pop's answer. "I couldn't agree more. Let's get to the bottom of this and terminate those responsible. No mercy on this, do you understand?"

We nod. Oh, we understand perfectly well.

The assholes responsible for killing so many people are about to be punished for their crimes.

CHAPTER 14

"That's the last of them," Shane says as he sets a box on the floor of the family room where we're all sitting, reading through old reports. There are seven moving-sized boxes stacked against the wall.

We're only one box in.

This is going to take a while.

"Some of these are just your grandmother's notes. Her thoughts," Ivie says as she stares down at a pile of papers in her lap. "She was so filled with grief."

"Yeah, and my aunt Claudia wasn't a prize," Carmine says with a wince. "I know, speaking ill of the dead and all, but she really wasn't. Pop said that Vinnie was a piece of shit, and he totally was. But Claudia wasn't much better. Maybe she was softer when she was young. I only knew her to be cold and brash."

"Elena definitely wasn't close to her," Rafe adds. "She hit the shit jackpot when it came to her parents."

"It's why she spent so much time with us." Shane sits on the floor next to Ivie and digs out some papers from the box. "She was always at our house. And in the summers, she came here to spend time with Gram. She's really more like a sister to us."

"Guys." I wave a pile of papers around. "I just found crime scene photos from the car wreck."

"Nice," Rafe says next to me. The others crowd around me as I lay the photos on a table, spreading them out so we can all look. "Man, that car was charred."

"Was it a Mercedes?" Ivie asks, squinting. "I think I see the logo in this picture."

"Yeah. Mercedes sedan." Rafe leans in to get a closer look, his hand on my shoulder. "So, she hit a tree?"

"Looks like it," Carmine says.

"And from what Gram said, the cops ruled it an accident."

I'm staring at one photo in particular. "You guys, this just doesn't look right. That tree is a good twenty yards from the road. How does she just veer off and hit it? Not to mention, there are no tire tracks on the road."

"You're right," Curt murmurs. "No tire tracks at all."

"Also, can we just talk about the fact that her front end isn't mangled?" Ivie asks. "If she hit the tree, and it set the car on fire, why isn't the front end totaled? It looks like someone just pushed it over to the tree and set it on fire."

"You think?" Carmine says bitterly. "Of course, they did. Like Pop said, she was murdered. This was no accident, and these photos prove it. Not that they prove much else."

"I'm going to keep looking at them," Ivie says thoughtfully. "Something else might pop out at me."

"Good idea." I return to my pile of papers and sit on the floor. "I could use some pizza while I do this."

"Same." Nadia reaches for her phone. "I'll order some in. Everyone tell me what they want."

"SHE SAVED EVERYTHING," Rafe says later after we've consumed four pizzas and made our way through two boxes. "For a woman who was so tight-lipped and didn't keep anything helpful in her office, she sure saved a lot of shit."

"I went through most of this before," Carmine adds. "But I just skimmed, looking for Elena's name since that was the focus. I should have been more thorough."

"You're one person," I remind him. "Now there's seven of us. We'll get through it."

"Your parents are here," Rafe says, checking his phone. "Security just texted me."

"Oh, I'll go say hi. I'll be right back."

I stand, jump over a box, and hurry from the room.

"Mama!" I rush over and pull my mom in for a hug. "You guys were supposed to be here yesterday."

"Your father had some things to wrap up," she says. "But we were very safe, don't worry. And we're here now."

"Where is Dad?" I ask, looking around.

"He's already off to find Igor and Carlo," Mom says, shaking her head. "He's eager to talk business."

"Typical." I loop my arm through hers. "You have a beautiful room upstairs."

"This is such a beautiful home," she replies. "I enjoyed being here for Nadia's wedding. I guess, if we have to be locked up somewhere, there are far worse places to be."

"No kidding. And you aren't exactly locked up. You just can't go anywhere without an escort."

She glances at me with eyes so much like mine and then giggles. "Yes, I see the difference. I'd like to get settled into our room and maybe take a little nap. You know what a nervous wreck I am on airplanes. I didn't get any rest at all."

"I know. You hate to fly. Well, you're here now." I show her up to her room, and once we've fussed over the beautiful décor and hug twice more, I leave her to nap.

But I'm not in a hurry to find the others. Not because we're working through all of the boxes of documents but because I could use a few minutes by myself.

I glance to my left and grin.

I'll just take a short walk through the yard.

The estate is beautiful and vast. Carlo's mother was a classy woman, and from what I gather, a little *extra.*

She loved fancy things, and that shines through in her home. Outside of museums, I've never seen so much artwork in my life. I'm afraid to touch anything. Rooms like the family room are comfortable to relax in, but other spaces are quite formal.

I'm sure it was a formidable place to host gatherings in. If she wanted to intimidate other families, all she had to do was invite them here.

I take a deep breath, sucking in the fresh air. It smells like it's going to rain, and if the dark clouds overhead are any indication, we'll have plenty of it by this evening.

But for now, the sun is still peeking through. I set off down a path that winds away from the house toward a row of trees.

I love being here. Even though we've only been in Seattle for a short time, it feels good. Like home. The air is fresh, and I just love how *green* everything is.

Not to mention, being with Rafe is a dream come true.

It was surreal last night, sitting in that room with Rafe's parents and Uncle Igor as if we did it all the time as a couple. Rafe even held my hand at one point. I almost jerked back, afraid that Uncle Igor would notice.

And then I remembered.

We can be together.

So much warmth and joy filled me at the thought, I was surprised it didn't radiate from me.

When I get to the edge of the trees, I'm surprised to find a tree house. And from the looks of it, it's pretty sturdy.

I glance around to see if anyone is watching.

I'm a grown woman. I have no business climbing up into a tree house.

I bite my lip.

"But it looks like fun," I mutter, and then decide... what the hell? Rafe and his brothers must have spent a lot of time up here when they were kids. And from what they said last night, it sounds like Elena played out here with them.

I wonder what they were like as kids? I grin as I reach the top of the ladder and step onto the platform.

I can just imagine Rafe running around here with a toy sword, playing pirate or space invaders with his siblings. I'm glad that he had the experience of growing up with a loving grandparent, and a safe haven to spend his summers.

I cross to the window and look outside at the grounds, surprised to see how far I wandered from the house.

It didn't feel that far when I walked over here.

The green grass is bright, and the house stands grandly a couple of hundred yards away.

I'm glad my parents arrived. I've been worried about them. All of them, actually. Someone out there has a vendetta against the mafia, and they're doing a good job of killing off entire families.

But why?

That's the question. Of course, every organization has done their fair share of bad things. You're friendly with some families and others you don't trust and can't stand.

But it's never *all of them.*

Is this someone who's been cast out of a family? Is this how they're taking their revenge?

I don't like it. And out here, by myself, I can admit that it scares the hell out of me. Because Rafe is a soldier in his organization. He'll go in with his brothers and do his best to kill the bad guys.

But, in the process, he could get killed himself. I suppose that's true every time he goes out on a mission for the family.

It's one of the reasons I always said I wouldn't marry someone connected to organized crime. I've seen too many women become widows far too young.

We've been lucky in my family. And the Martinellis have been fortunate, as well.

But when will that luck change?

"I don't want to find out." I take another deep breath. "And I can't help who I love. I tried to deny it for years. I told myself that Rafe was lost to me and that it was for the best. But it was *never* for the best. Because all I did was long for him. I married Richard, hoping that I could fall in love with someone else and be happy.

"And we all know where that got me."

I swallow hard and watch as the first fat drops start to fall from the sky.

"I'm done denying what my heart and head both tell me is right. Rafe is it for me. And I'm finally with him. The fact that he's very much a part of his mafia family is just something I'll have to learn to live with. And, for the immediate future, we have to figure out who's trying to kill us and stay alive."

I refuse to be a widow before he's even asked me to marry him.

I yawn and then frown when I hear someone yelling my name. I glance around and narrow my eyes when I see Rafe running over the grass, calling for me.

"Hey!" I wave out the window and smile when he sees me. But he doesn't look happy in the least.

He runs over to the tree house, faster than I've ever seen anyone move in my life. He lifts his phone to his mouth, but I can't hear what he says.

And when he reaches me, he quickly climbs up, rushes over, and yanks me into his arms.

He's panting, gasping for air.

"Hey, what happened? Rafe, what's wrong?"

"We couldn't find you." He pulls back and frames my face in his hands. "Jesus Christ, A, don't do that to me ever again. You scared the shit out of me."

"I didn't go far."

"What if someone had nabbed you?"

"I'm *right here.*"

He just rocks us back and forth, clinging to me.

"I just got you back in my life. I can't lose you again. Now or ever."

"Funny." I turn my face and kiss his chest. "I was just thinking the same. I want to wrap this all up so we can get on with our lives. And I need us both to live through it."

"We will."

"Promise."

"I promise. I have no intention of being apart from you again. And the next time you want to go for a walk, just let me know, and I'll go with you."

"I wanted a few minutes alone," I reply and then snort when he scowls as if I've hurt his feelings. "We're allowed to have a few moments alone now and again. It's healthy."

"Then just warn me so I'm not off on a frantic wild goose chase."

"Deal. I didn't mean to scare you, Rafe."

"I know. Hey, are you ever going to call me Rocco?"

I laugh and lead him to the ladder. "Hell, no."

"Why?" He's not mad now. He's just grinning. He knows the answer to this.

"Because *Rocco* is a meathead's name. And you're no meathead."

"I kinda am, honey."

"No." I bounce down to the ground and wait for

him to join me so I can plant a kiss on his cheek. "You aren't. Everyone else in the world can call you Rocco for all I care, but your name is *Rafe*. So that's what I'll call you."

"Fine."

"Do you really hate it that much?"

"No, but I have a reputation to uphold here. Rocco sounds tougher. I need people to think I'm a badass."

"We all know you're a badass." He takes my hand and leads me back to the path so we can walk back to the house. "But you're not badass with me. You're sweet and gentle. Sexy. Everything."

"I like that last word the best."

I glance up and grin. "Yeah? Well, it's true. Besides, it would sound weird if I called you Rocco."

"Try it."

"Hey, Rocco, will you pass me the chips?"

He thinks about it and then starts laughing. "Okay, yeah. It sounds dumb when you say it."

"See? Told you."

"I'm hungry."

"We literally just had pizza."

"Yeah, but then I thought you were missing and used up about two thousand calories in adrenaline. I think there's some pepperoni left."

"Let's go find it, then."

CHAPTER 15

~RAFE~

"*J* thought it would be easier today with fresh eyes," I mumble as I sit on the couch, Annika next to me, and another pile of papers in my lap. "It's not. Still boring as fuck."

"Drink more coffee," Ivie suggests.

"I never thought *fuck* was boring," Nadia says, her eyes narrowed thoughtfully as she sips her coffee. "I mean, if you're doing it right."

I shake my head. "Carmine, control your woman."

Nadia's face splits into a slow grin. "Yeah, Carmine. Control your woman."

"She'll kill you, man," Carmine says to me with a sigh. "Don't provoke her."

"Did anyone ever go talk to this Danvers guy?" Curt asks out of the blue. He looks up from the page he's been reading and frowns. "It says here that John Danvers killed Vinnie, but so far, I haven't heard any of you mention any research into that dude. No personal investigator interviews or anything."

"I don't know," Shane says, shaking his head.

"I'll go talk to him. Where is he?"

"Hold on," Ivie says as she taps on the keys of her laptop, which is always nearby. "He's at a maximum-security prison in Walla Walla. On death row."

"Who do we know that can get in there to have a little chat with Danvers?"

"Wait." Annika rests her hand on my arm. "I don't think it's a good idea for you to go into a prison to see a killer."

I blink down at her. "Why not?"

"Because he's a *killer*, Rafe."

"He's in *prison*," I reply. "It's not like I'm going to pose as an inmate and try to talk to him on the inside, for God's sake."

"I don't like it," she whispers with a mutinous scowl on her gorgeous face.

"Hey." I take her chin in my hand and lean in to kiss her. "I'll be fine."

"Who do we know who can get Rocco into the prison?" Shane asks.

"Archer's cousin, Matt Montgomery, might be someone to talk to," Carmine says. "He's a top cop in Seattle and probably has connections."

"Let's call Archer."

I pull my phone out of my pocket and put the call

through to Elena's husband. He answers after the second ring.

"Hey, Rocco, what's up?"

"I have a question for you. Do you think your cousin Matt would speak with me?"

He's quiet for a second. "I guess that depends on what you want to talk about."

"We're doing some digging into Elena's parents' deaths," I say, quickly filling him in. "I'd like to go speak to Danvers in person. But you can't just show up to a maximum-security prison and ask to speak to someone on death row, you know?"

"Makes sense. I'm sure Matt would talk to you, especially about this. Let me give him a call and give him your number."

"Excellent. Thanks, man. Let him know he can call anytime."

"Will do."

He hangs up, and I rub my hands together. "This doesn't suck. This is a *plan*. I can't just sit here and read old notes. It's making me crazy. Is anyone else hungry?"

"Mom's making breakfast burritos," Annika says. "She'll call out for us when they're ready."

"Your mom can *cook*," Ivie says with a grin. "I'm so glad she's here."

"Me, too."

My phone rings in my hand, surprising me. "That was fast. Hi, Matt, this is Rocco."

"Archer filled me in on what's going on. I have a

buddy who used to work with us here at the force who moved to Walla Walla a few years ago. His wife's family is there. Anyway, he's the warden at that facility. I'm sure I can get you in."

"Can we make it happen today?"

"I'll give him a call and ask. Are you driving over? It's a long way."

"I'll take the helicopter."

"Would you mind if I rode with you? I'd like to observe your interview. I work homicide now, and I'd be interested to hear what he has to say."

"Doesn't bother me at all, especially if your friend can help me out."

"I'll call you back as soon as I know anything. I can be ready to leave in about an hour."

"Great."

I click off just as Annika's mom walks into the room carrying a big tray heaping with steaming breakfast burritos.

"We could have come fetched these," Curt says, jumping up to take the heavy tray from her.

"You're busy," she says with a smile. "I'll be right back with some plates and stuff."

She bustles out and quickly returns with all kinds of condiments.

"This is like a delicious buffet," I mutter, my stomach growling. Before I can take even one bite, my phone rings again.

"Rocco."

"It's Matt. We're good to go. Just tell me where to meet you."

~

THE SMALL AIRSTRIP outside of Walla Walla is only a couple of miles from the prison. There's a car there, and a tall, dark-haired man waiting for us.

"Montgomery," he says with a smile as he walks toward us. He puts his hand out to shake Matt's. "It's damn good to see you."

"You, too," Matt says with a smile. "You look great, Middleton."

"Yeah, well, it's the armpit of the state here, but the wife's happy." He shrugs and turns to me. "You must be Martinelli."

"That's right." I shake his hand. "Thank you for letting us come today."

"Matt's an old friend. It's not a problem. I'll drive you over."

We all pile into the car, Middleton in the driver's seat and Matt next to him. I'm in the back, which I don't mind because I can get the lay of the land around us.

It's flat. Not much to see. And certainly nowhere for someone to hide, should they escape.

"Couple of things to remember when you get inside," Middleton says. "First, we'll take your weapons off your hands and return them to you when you're ready to leave. Next, this guy's an asshole. He's not physically violent, but he has a mouth on him. He'll be secured to the chair, unable to move about the room. Matt and I will be on the other side of the observation glass, and we have three armed guards on standby should he decide to *get* physically violent."

"Has anyone else come to see him since he's been in?" I ask.

"Not a one," Middleton replies. "In the nine years he's been a guest at our beautiful resort, he's had no visitors, no calls. No mail. He doesn't send anything out."

"I have Ivie doing a background search on him," I murmur. "My sister-in-law is good at research. So, to clarify, he's had no contact with the outside world at all in nine years?"

"That's right."

"Interesting."

"It's not unusual," Middleton continues. "These guys are the shitbags of society, Rocco. They've not only murdered. Many of them are rapists, have killed family members, and did all sorts of despicable crap that embarrassed their families. Hurt them. They don't have loved ones. They gave that up long ago."

"But I've heard about women who get off on establishing relationships with dudes on death row," I say. "Do you get much of that here?"

"Yeah, some of the guys get letters now and then. I

don't get it. But we don't have anyone married to someone they met while on the inside here."

"No conjugal visits?"

"Hell, no. Not on death row. Besides, these aren't the kind of guys most women want to fuck, you know what I mean?"

My stomach hardens.

Middleton pulls into his parking slot, and we walk through three sets of secure, heavy doors. Matt and I are relieved of our weapons, and we walk through metal detectors. I have to sign a book and a waiver.

Before long, we're walking down an institutional-looking hallway lined with doors. The walls are grey. The floor is grey. It smells of disinfectant.

I guess death row isn't supposed to be pleasant.

"You're in here," Middleton says and then points to the door just three feet to the left. "And we're in here. The armed guards are in with you. If, at any time, you don't feel comfortable, just say so and you can leave."

"Jesus, is he going to try to eat my face or something?"

"We never know with these assholes." Middleton sighs. "You can go in."

I'm not one to stereotype. I didn't have any preconceived notions when I walked in here today regarding what this Danvers would look like.

But when I walk through the door, the man sitting at the table is pretty much what I would expect when I think *murderer*.

He's probably fifty but looks much older than that with wrinkled skin covered in tattoos from his hairline to the tips of his fingers. His brown eyes are hard and cold. His hair's a long, tangled mess.

And when I sit across from him, he simply stares at me.

"Did they tell you who I am?" I ask.

"No."

"I'm Rocco Martinelli. I'm here to talk to you because you were convicted of killing Vinnie Watkins nine years ago."

He doesn't say anything, just stares at me.

"Vinnie was my uncle by marriage. I'd like to talk to you about the circumstances surrounding the case."

"Read the fucking case files," he says.

"I don't want to. I want to talk to *you*." I don't lean forward. I don't even blink. "I want to know who hired you to kill Vinnie."

His impassive face doesn't even twitch. "I don't have to tell you shit."

"Nope. You don't have to. But you're already here, man. It's over. More people are dying. Three bosses killed last week. And their families."

Now, his eyes narrow in interest.

"When we started looking at the big picture, it seemed like these recent murders are similar to when Vinnie and his wife died."

"Been a long time," Danvers says.

"Yeah. A long time. And in this business, people

have long memories. So, I'd like to ask you, man to man, who hired you?"

"I ain't in your business, man. Maybe my memory ain't so good."

"I think your memory is just fine."

He watches me and seems to think it over. And just when I think he's not going to say any more, he sighs and starts to talk.

"Didn't nobody hire me. I didn't kill him."

I scoff, but Danvers shakes his head with impatience. "I'm telling you, I didn't kill 'im. I ain't got nothing to lose here, man. I was his cellmate. Vinnie was a stupid piece of shit. Ran his mouth, thought his shit didn't stink. Let me tell you, it did. He thought he was too good to be in here, but he got caught doing some shady shit, you know? Anyway, I didn't like the fucker, but I was only in for a couple of years, got caught sellin' some dope. Not a huge amount, just enough to get me a couple years, you know?"

Now that he's started talking, he won't shut up. And he says *you know* after every other sentence. But it's fucking fascinating.

"So, one morning, I wake up, and Vinnie's dead in his bunk. Bled through the mattress, too. Fucker. And I banged on the bars to get the guard's attention. Next thing I know, I'm being hauled off to isolation, and then I'm standing trial for killin' the son of a bitch. I dealt. I admit that. I was into some bad shit. But I ain't never killed nobody, you know?"

"Did you tell the public defender all of this?"

"Sure, but nobody wanted to listen to me. They wouldn't even let me testify on the stand on my behalf. Said it would look bad to the jury. Instead, the mother-fucker lawyer they gave me just sat back on his hands and let the DA tell the jury what a jerk I was, presented evidence that wasn't true, and then I'm sentenced to die. Here I am."

I narrow my eyes at him. "John, are you telling me *no one* ever contacted you about Vinnie, about who he was, and asked you to kill him or offered to pay you to kill him?"

"Fuck no. I have a daughter. Ain't seen her in a dozen years now. Won't ever again. I was supposed to get out. Get clean. Be a dad. I wouldn't have killed nobody."

I sit back, stunned at this turn of events. Could he be lying? Possibly. But my gut tells me no.

"Thank you for telling me all of this. For being straight with me."

"You're the asshole's family. I guess you should know the real story. Not that it does any good now."

"You'd be surprised. And, John, if I can prove this and get everything resolved, we're going to work on getting you out of here and back with your daughter."

His eyes light up for a nanosecond but then dull again. "Won't work. Thanks for sayin' that, but it won't work."

"We'll see." I stand and nod at him. "We'll see about

that."

I leave the room and meet up with Matt and Middleton in the hallway.

"What do you think?" I ask Matt as I rub my hand over the back of my neck.

"I don't think he's lying," Matt says slowly. "I've interviewed a shit-ton of suspects in my time, and the liars don't tend to give up that much information. He looked you in the eye. And when you said you'd help him, he looked...hopeful."

"Agreed," Middleton says. "I've never seen him like that. And if he's here because someone dirty put him here, that'll piss me the fuck off."

"I'm going to keep digging," I reply. "They may have already found something else back home while I've been gone."

"If you find any other reasons to believe that Danvers is innocent, you get the information to me," Matt says. "And I'll help get it to the people who can help him."

"Will do."

THE FLIGHT back is uneventful and quiet, with Matt and I both lost in our thoughts. Once back at Gram's place, I hurry in to check in with the others.

Carmine smashes a soda can in his hand after I recount the interview.

"Someone fucking set him up," Carmine growls.

"I mean, that's not shocking," Nadia points out. "It happens."

"Not like this," Shane disagrees. "We don't send innocent people to death row. We don't involve civilians in organization business."

"Sometimes, there are casualties," Igor says, thinking it over. "But, no, it's not something we like to do."

"I want to know who the fuck set up that man for killing Vinnie," Pop says, his eyes hard as steel. "Because I'm going to kill them with my own hands."

"I might know something," Ivie says, surprising us all. "Right before Rafe got home, I was doing some digging on the Danvers' trial. The judge was one Honorable Lawrence Santiago. He'd been a judge in Washington for only three years at the time. Relocated here from Florida."

"Okay," Pop says, frowning. "And?"

"Well, at first, it ended there. It's pretty weird to only have three years' history on a forty-something-year-old man. So, I peeled back some layers. Turns out, Lawrence P. Santiago is actually Santiago-Reyes. The brother of Phillipe Reyes. Of Miami."

Pop's eyes narrow. "Of the Reyes organization."

"That's right," Ivie says. "He has ties to the mafia family in Miami."

"Looks like we're headed to Miami in the morning," I say. "Get packed."

CHAPTER 16

~ANNIKA~

"*I* called ahead," Shane says after we land in Miami. "And I just heard back from Maceo, Phillipe's son. He said he's at the hospital, and we can meet him there."

Rafe and Carmine share a look.

"Why are they at the hospital?" I ask.

"Looks like we're about to go find out," Nadia says. "And I don't have a good feeling about this."

Because of traffic, it takes more than an hour to reach the hospital. When we all file out of the car, we find a dark-haired, dark-skinned man approaching with a grim look on his face. When he sees me, he does a double-take but then shakes his head and addresses Carmine.

"I have a waiting room set up for us inside," he says by way of greeting. "I don't want any trouble today."

"You won't get any trouble," Carmine says to the other underboss. "We just have questions."

Maceo nods and leads the six of us inside to a waiting room on the second floor, where three other men wait. When he closes the door, he turns to us.

"What is this about?"

"First, why are you at the hospital?" Carmine asks, and Maceo narrows his eyes.

"You don't know?"

"No, we've been on a plane most of the morning. Miami's pretty far away from Seattle," Rafe says.

"My father was killed this morning," Maceo replies. "My mother is in intensive care with multiple stab wounds. My young sister is on the run with her Godfather because we don't know who did this or what the motive is."

I shake my head and turn to Ivie, who slips her hand into mine.

"Fucking hell," Carmine growls. "Jesus, I'm sorry, Maceo. We hadn't heard."

"Ours is the fourth family targeted," Maceo says.

"Fifth," Shane says. "We have reason to believe this began more than a decade ago with Vinnie and Claudia Watkins."

Shane briefly fills the other man in and then says, "Where is Lawrence Reyes? The man who goes by Santiago? And why was he working in our city?"

Maceo scowls. "My father's brother?"

"That's the one," Carmine says.

"My family hasn't had anything to do with that asshole in twenty years. He's a traitor. He was feeding information back and forth to the Carlito family in Dallas. Working both sides."

"But the Carlitos haven't been active for many years," Carmine says.

"If you think that family has been sleeping all these years, you're an idiot," Maceo says, cutting to the chase. "They've been quiet, but they're not asleep. I don't know what they had on my uncle or why he decided to start working for them. It was the biggest disgrace of my father's life. Everyone told my father to kill Lawrence, but he couldn't do it. He gave his brother an ultimatum. If he wouldn't stop working for the Carlitos, he was no longer welcome here.

"He left the next day, and no one has heard from him since. I don't know why he was working in Seattle."

"He was the *judge* on the case of the man accused of killing Vinnie," Rafe tells him.

"I've honestly told you everything I know." Maceo stops and glances over at me, looking like he wants to say something, but then turns back to Rafe. "The Carlitos are dirty as hell, man. If they're behind all of these assassinations, they need to be taken out."

"I have a feeling we'll be headed to Dallas in the morning," Carmine says.

"I'd like to go with you," Maceo says.

"You have your hands full here," Shane points out.

"With your father dead and your mother in the ICU. Not to mention, you're now the boss of your organization, Maceo. Let us go take care of this. We will keep you informed every step of the way."

"I don't like sending someone else in to clean up my mess," Maceo says.

"It's our mess, too. Has been for a damn long time," Carmine replies. "It's going to be handled."

Maceo nods and gestures to me as we turn to leave. "I'd like to talk to you."

"Me?" I point at myself and then glance behind me.

"Yes, you." He pins the others with dark brown eyes. "Alone."

"Fuck that," Rafe says, pushing me behind him. "If you have business with her, you have business with *me*."

"Hey." I pat Rafe's shoulder and smile when he looks down at me. "Just wait right outside the door. You're right here. Nothing's going to happen."

"No."

"I only want to have a private word. I mean her no harm. I give you my word," Maceo says.

Finally, Rafe nods once and steps outside the door but watches through the little window.

"He's in love with you," Maceo says.

"Yeah. What's up?" I ask.

"I want you to know that I've received emails from an unknown source. They contained photos. Of you."

I narrow my eyes as the blood leaves my face, and my heart hammers.

"I didn't know you at all until you got out of that car. I only recognized you from the photos. Someone is trying to ruin your reputation, and the reputation of the Tarenkov family. What you do with this information is up to you."

"What did you do with the photos?"

"I deleted them." His eyes harden. "We don't hurt women, Annika. I have no beef with you or your family. Therefore, I have no reason to keep them. But I can't tell you where they were sent from."

"Do you know if they were sent to other families?"

"No, I don't know."

I nod and offer him a small smile. "Thanks for letting me know."

"Good luck to you."

"Same to you. And I really am sorry for your loss."

I slip out the door and join the others in the hallway.

"What the fuck did he want?" Rafe demands, but I just shake my head.

"Not here."

"Let's check into the hotel and decide what we want to do from there," Carmine suggests.

"So, all this time, it's been the Carlito family," Nadia says as she kicks off her shoes and drops into a sofa in her suite.

"They're involved," Carmine agrees. "How deeply, we don't know quite yet. But we're going to find out."

"Obviously, we can't tell them we're headed to Dallas," Shane says. "We're going to sneak in and infiltrate their headquarters. Or their compound."

"I've been looking at satellite images," Ivy says. "It looks like a compound similar to your grandmother's place in Seattle."

"It'd better not be that nice, or we'll never get inside." Rafe pushes his hand through his hair in agitation. "We need to call Pop."

"Yeah." Carmine sighs warily and picks up his phone. "I'll FaceTime him."

Carmine dials, and when Carlo picks up the phone, Carmine fills him in on the details.

"Igor and I will meet you in Dallas tomorrow morning," Carlo says.

"Why?" Shane asks. "We have plenty of manpower here. We can get in and out and be done."

"Because this vendetta has been a long time coming," Carlo says. "And I'm going to look those people in the eye when they're questioned—and when they're killed."

"We can't talk you out of this." Carmine's statement isn't a question.

"No. We'll meet you there. I'll message you to coordinate the time."

"Yes, sir," Carmine says. "I'll talk to you soon."

He ends the call and shakes his head.

"This will put a wrench in things," Ivie says. "If Igor and Carlo are there, not only do we have to do the job, but we also have to look out for them."

"Look at you," Nadia says to Ivie, a proud smile on her face. "Sounding all mobster-like and stuff."

"I know, right?" Ivie asks.

"Yeah, it's going to switch it up," Rafe agrees. "We won't infiltrate anything. We'll be knocking on the fucking front door."

"Sometimes, that's not a bad strategy," Carmine says, thinking it over. "They still don't know that we're coming. Maybe we make it seem like it's a friendly call."

"I'm not feeling particularly friendly toward the Carlitos," Rafe says.

"But they don't know that, do they? We'll make it seem like we're just after some information. Because we need that, too. And then, we'll see what happens."

"I don't like it," Shane says and crosses his arms over his chest. "Something still feels off. Like we're missing a piece."

"Curt's still going through paperwork in Seattle," Ivie reminds her husband. "Maybe he'll come up with something between now and tomorrow morning."

"He's flying to Dallas with the dads," Carmine says. "We'll need him."

"And then he's done working for the family," Shane adds. "This isn't what he signed on to do when he asked to work for me. He's my ranch manager. He's done after this."

"We have no issue with that," Carmine replies.

"OH MY GOD, I'm so *tired.*" I collapse onto the massive king-sized bed in our bedroom and long for a nap. "I feel like we've been up for weeks."

"What did he say to you?"

I crack an eye and stare at Rafe, who's standing at the end of the bed. "Huh?"

"What did Maceo say to you, Annika?"

"Oh." I take a second to take stock of how I feel about this. Turns out, I'm not embarrassed. Or even sad. I'm just pissed off.

I sit up and lick my lips. "He received emails from an unknown sender that had photos attached. Of me. The photos from before."

Rafe's hands ball into fists.

"He was warning me that someone sent them and was trying to ruin my reputation. My family's reputation. Honestly, I think he handled it really well. Discreetly. And he seemed really pissed about it. He said that he doesn't believe in hurting women."

"Son of a bitch." Rafe paces away and shoves his

hands into his pockets, then stares out the window to the ocean beyond.

"Why are you mad at me?" I climb off the bed and prop my hands on my hips.

"I'm not." He doesn't raise his voice.

"You're acting mad. I didn't do anything wrong, *remember?*"

"What do you want from me?" Rafe spins and holds his hands out at his sides. "What do you expect? Of course, I'm pissed. Someone is dicking with the woman I love. Someone is trying to *hurt* you, and I don't know who it is. I thought we had this handled with the Boston thing, but I guess not. And now it's just one more thing to pile onto everything else that's happening around us."

"Well, I'm sorry that I'm such an inconvenience. I didn't plan on this, you know. It's *never* good timing to find out some asshole has intimate photos of you and plans to share them with the world. But I guess I could have put out a notice on social media and asked them to hold off for a few weeks while we clean up this other mess."

I stomp into the bathroom and slam the door shut.

He just makes me so *mad* sometimes.

"Annika."

"I need a second." I lean my hands on the bathroom vanity and take a deep breath as Rafe opens the door and steps inside. "What if I'd been on the toilet?"

"I don't care." He pulls me to him and wraps his big

arms around my shoulders. "I'm sorry I'm a monstrous dickhole."

"You really are."

He kisses my head. "I know. And for the record, I'm not mad at you. I really am just pissed at whoever is still jerking you around. I want it finished. All of it."

"Yeah." I finally loop my arms around him and hug him back. "I'm not even embarrassed about it anymore. It just is what it is. And we'll figure out who's behind it. It's like they're a high school bully who leaves mostly naked photos of the popular girl on all of the lockers as a joke."

"No one ever left a naked photo on my locker," he says with a pout. "I feel left out."

"Perv." I lean my head back and pucker my lips. He doesn't disappoint with the kiss he lays on me. "Thanks for being outraged on my behalf."

"I wasn't kidding before," he says. "Someone is trying to hurt you. And I love you. That means they have to die."

"You love me?"

He frowns and then scoffs. "Of course, I love you. Have I been alone the past few weeks?"

"You haven't said it." I snuggle closer and nuzzle my nose into the crook of his neck. "And for the record, I love you, too. I always have, Rafe. I pushed you away, over and over again, but all along, I knew you were the one for me. There will never be anyone else for me."

"That's a good thing."

"Really?" I raise a brow. "Or what?"

"You don't want to know." He slings me over his shoulder and carries me to the bed, my head coming inches from hitting the doorframe.

"You almost just killed me."

"Nah, I missed by a mile."

I laugh and then squeal when he drops me unceremoniously onto the mattress.

"You're totally a caveman."

"Yes. Rocco carry Annika."

I giggle and scurry away when he reaches for me.

"I need a hot shower and some food. I'm starving. Then you can have your way with me."

"I think we need a compromise in this situation," Rafe says.

"No. I said what I said."

"How are we supposed to have any kind of healthy relationship if you're not willing to grow and respect our differences of opinion?"

I shake my head at him. "Why do you sound like a shrink now? I'm getting in the shower."

"Fine. If you love shower time that much, I'll compromise with *you* and wash your back. I'll even let you stand in the hot water so you don't get too cold. I'm a giver."

"You're weird this afternoon." I laugh and bounce out of his grasp as I hurry back to the bathroom. "And I don't need you to shower with me."

"Stop begging. It's embarrassing. I already told you I'd shower with you."

"You're such a pain in the ass."

"But I'm *your* pain in the ass." He pulls me to him, the laughter fading as he lowers his lips to mine. "And I'm going to make you forget your name tonight, my love."

"Well, when you put it like that, I guess you can shower with me."

"Great. Will you *share* the hot water spray?"

"You said I could have it."

"Don't be selfish. It's all about compromise, remember?"

"I'm reserving water privileges until I see how good of a job you do at washing my back."

"Oh, honey, I'm *very* good. There's no need to worry about that."

CHAPTER 17

"It's still dark," I whisper when Rafe kisses my neck and drags his hand down my arm. I was lost in a very pleasant dream, and I'm not ready to wake up. "Not morning yet."

"We have to get an early start," he reminds me, his voice thick with sleep. "Big day today."

"Five more minutes." I burrow my face into the pillow, but he kisses down my bare spine, and little licks of pleasure spark over my skin, making the dream slip from my mind and all of my attention shift to Rafe. The man is insatiable. It's like he just can't get enough of me.

I'm not complaining.

Making love with Rafe Martinelli is the delight of my life.

As I turn over to face him, the covers slip down, and the cool air from our room blows over my skin. The combination of cool air and Rafe's warm skin send goose bumps over me, waking me fully from sleep. My legs tangle with his, and his already-hard cock presses to my thigh impressively.

"How are you already awake and ready for this?"

"Need you," he whispers against my neck. "More than I need to breathe."

"I'm right here." I skim my nose over his shoulder and sigh in delight when his rough hand closes over my breast. His thumb brushes back and forth over my nipple, making it come to life.

It's a slow, sweet coupling, full of heavy sighs and light nibbles. Whispers.

And just as he teases my already-slick opening with the head of his cock, he looks into my eyes, the first light of dawn casting grey over his face. "You're everything I've ever wanted. All I've ever needed, A."

Slowly, so slowly I have to bite my lip, he slides inside me and frames my face with his hands. I can feel the emotion coming off him in waves, and it absolutely takes my breath away.

"Your heart matches mine," I reply softly and take one of his hands in both of mine, linking our fingers as I hold his gaze. "We're linked, *bonded*. Together. And no matter what life throws at us, that will never change, Rafe."

"God, I love you so much." His mouth closes over mine, and his hips begin moving. But nothing about our joining is rushed. Nothing is urgent. It's the purest form of lovemaking there is. As intimate as it gets.

When we were young, we made love often, lost in each other. But now that we have our second chance, it's so much…more.

More intense.

More meaningful.

"Mine," he whispers. "Open your eyes."

I comply and find him watching me with those fiery blue depths.

"You're mine, Annika. Today and every day that I walk this Earth. You're the only one for me. Do you understand?"

"Of course, I understand. Because I feel exactly the same." My hand dives into his hair, my fingers tangling in the strands as I hold on, enjoying every moment with this man that I love so much.

With his forehead pressed to mine, he picks up speed and sends us both over that delicious crest into oblivion, where I feel so connected to him, I'm not sure where I end and he begins.

We are one.

We always have been.

"Mine," he says again before kissing me so tenderly, it brings tears to my eyes. "Why are you crying?"

"Because I thought this, you, were lost to me. And this is all the sweeter because of it."

"I'm never letting you go again," he promises and kisses my hand. "Ever. If something were to happen, and our families forbade it, we'd leave them. I will *not* be without you, Annika. I can't. I lived through that torture for far longer than any man should have to. I'll do everything in my power to always have you by my side."

"I know." I kiss him sweetly. "I know it. And I'm right here with you. Nothing's ever going to tear us apart again."

He rolls to the side, unlinking us, and then pads into the bathroom.

"Sun's coming up," he calls as he starts the shower. "Pop wants to get an early start."

"Yeah." I sigh, a little sad that our wonderful moment is over. But there will be more.

A lifetime of moments, just like this one and better.

"I want to talk a bit about today before we're with the others," Rafe says as he pokes his head out of the bathroom.

"Okay. What's up?"

"I want you on the periphery of everything that happens today. If you can stay in the van, all the better. I don't want you to see any action."

I frown, but he keeps talking.

"I'm not saying that to sound sexist. Yes, you can shoot—probably better than I can. And you're damn smart. But you haven't trained for these situations. You're a doctor. A damn good one."

"Now you're just buttering me up so I say, '*Yes, sir.*'"

"No. I'm not saying anything that isn't completely

true." Steam starts billowing out of the bathroom from the hot shower. "These are dangerous people, A."

"I'm well aware of that."

"Nothing can happen to you."

"Likewise." I stand from the bed, also stark-naked, and prop my hand on my hip. "We have the same goal, Rafe. To get in and out alive while making sure the target is eliminated."

"I don't want you in the middle of it."

"Too late. I *am* in the middle of it. And I'll be surrounded by people who have far more experience than I do. I won't do anything to put anyone in harm's way. I'm not careless. This may not be my specialty, but Tarenkov blood runs through my veins. I can handle myself."

"You stick close to Curt or Nadia. You keep your weapon on you at all times, and don't be afraid to use it. And, Annika, I'm only going to say this one time... If something happens to me, you absolutely *cannot* jump into the middle of things out of pure emotion. You'll instinctively want to run to me, help me, but you will only put yourself in danger. Keep that cool head of yours on straight. It'll keep you alive."

I blow out a long breath, the thought of something happening to Rafe turning my blood cold.

"I'll keep my head on straight," I promise him. "But, Rafe, if something happens to you, I'll never forgive you."

He walks to me and pulls me into his arms, rocking

us back and forth. "It's just a what-if, baby. I want you to be prepared for anything, and I need you to stay safe. That's *my* primary objective today. To keep you absolutely safe."

"I love you." My words are a whisper against his chest. The thought of *anything* happening to Rafe fills me with absolute terror. I don't think I would survive losing him again.

"I love you, too." He kisses my forehead. "Let's get ready to go. Pop's impatient."

"I'm surprised that he wants to go on this mission," I admit as I follow Rafe into the bathroom. "It's not that he and Uncle Igor are out of shape. Quite the opposite, actually. But they don't *have* to do this anymore."

"It's personal for them. I don't know all of the details yet, but that's the feeling I get. I suspect that when we're all together, they'll fill us in on everything they know. I don't know about Igor, but I know Pop can take care of himself. He's a big man, but he moves surprisingly fast, and he's deadly with a weapon. From what I understand, he was formidable in his prime."

"I've heard that Uncle Igor was the same."

"That would make sense. They're two of the most powerful men in this country."

He gets in the shower as I brush out my hair and tie it up on top of my head so it doesn't get wet when I step in.

"Now that Carmine and Nadia are married, and they were each next in line to be the boss of our respective families, what will happen if something happens to either Carlo or Uncle Igor?"

Rafe goes quiet for a moment.

"I think the two families are now merged. Considered one family. Nadia and Carmine would head both organizations."

"Holy hell, that's a lot of power."

"Yes."

I open the glass door and join him.

"Want me to wash your back again?" He grins and waggles his eyebrows.

"Good God, you're insatiable. We literally *just* finished."

"That was round one. I've had time to rest."

"No. You said yourself. Your father is impatient."

He pulls me to him, wet and slippery. "A few more minutes won't matter."

"They're already here," Shane says, pointing to the other private jet sitting on the jetway.

"Just arrived," Rafe confirms. "We were only twenty minutes behind them."

Shane's phone rings, and he answers right away. "This is Shane. Yep. We see you. We'll be right over."

He hangs up and turns to the rest of us.

"Pop wants all of us to go over there for a briefing. That jet is bigger, and our only office in Dallas."

"Makes sense," Carmine says as we come to a stop. We leave all of our belongings on the plane—one of the perks of being on a private aircraft—and hurry over to the much larger jet where everyone else is waiting.

Carlo and Igor are seated at a table on one side. Curt's in a chair with his laptop open on a small table. The six of us file in and find seats, all business, all ready for what's about to come.

"This could be the most important day in our organization's—or *any* organization's—existence," Carlo begins. "Igor and I have been doing some research on the Carlito family for several months on the down-low. We had to be careful and methodical because this family seems to have eyes and ears *everywhere*."

"They are sneaky," Igor adds. "And more intelligent than any of us gave them credit for, for many years. To our detriment. There's still much we don't know. We will not just burst in, guns blazing."

"We want answers," Carlo picks up. "We want to ask questions and get answers."

"We'll get them."

We all turn in surprise at the sound of Mick Sergi's voice. The New York boss steps onto the plane, his son Billy right behind him.

"What are you doing here?" Carmine demands, but Carlo holds up a hand.

"Thank you for coming," Carlo says and then nods again when Maceo from Miami follows the Sergis onto the plane. "I'm sorry for your loss, Maceo."

Maceo's eyes are hard and cold.

"Thank you."

"Please explain this," Carmine says as he pulls his sidearm from its holster and lays it on a table.

"All of our personal beefs with each other, whether big or small, are set aside for today," Igor says, watching the others. "Our only vendetta, our only focus, is destroying the Carlito family. But we have to get answers before we kill them."

"So, what's the plan?" Rafe asks. "We just march up to the front door and ring the bell?"

"Precisely," Carlo says, smiling at his son. "My three sons and I will ring the bell. Say we're there to talk, to ask questions. Be non-threatening."

"In the meantime," Igor says, "the rest of us will infiltrate the perimeter and take out their security."

"It's damn good security," Curt says, still staring at his computer. "I have it up on the laptop, thanks to a late-night email from Ivie."

"Wasn't easy to find," Ivie mutters with a mutinous frown. "Bastards."

"I have a plan in place, and I'll go over it with everyone," Curt says and nods at Carlo.

"Excellent. While my boys and I are talking with Benji inside, you'll all take out Benji's men. And once inside, Igor, Mick, and Maceo will have plenty of time to get more answers before extinguishing the Carlitos and their bloodline. They will never be an issue for any organization ever again."

"How do we know that they're behind *everything*?" Nadia asks thoughtfully.

"They're the common denominator," Mick replies. "Crime families own up to what they do. If I have a beef with someone and have them killed, I'll admit it. I don't hide. No one claimed to have issues with any of the families killed over the past few weeks. *No one.*"

"And the Carlitos haven't said a word," Igor adds.

"How many Carlitos are there?" Ivie asks. "We've only heard of Benji. We know he's young, only in his early twenties, and his father didn't have an interest in the family business after his grandfather died."

"We know that Benji is trying to run things." Mick rolls his eyes. "He's a fucking *kid*. His grandfather died twenty-five years ago."

"Who's Benji's father?" Carmine asks.

"Francisco," Carlo says. "Francisco Carlito. He was never one to be in the forefront of things. Happy to sit in his father's shadow. And when his father died, we all assumed the family went to sleep."

"They never slept," Maceo says. "They're just good at working underground."

"Is Francisco dead?" Ivie asks.

"We think so," Igor says. "We believe that Francisco's death is what propelled Benji into action."

"But it's not been confirmed that Francisco is dead." Rafe crosses his arms. "There are too many unanswered questions."

"That's what today is for," Carlo reminds him.

"Now, Curt, tell us your plan for getting inside and ambushing their security, and let's finish this mission."

"I DON'T LIKE THIS." I'm sitting between Ivie and Nadia in the van, ready to jump out and set Curt's plan into motion.

It's a damn good scheme.

We watch as the four men walk down a driveway and up onto a wide front porch.

"Is it just me, or does something feel off?"

"It's not just you," Ivie says.

"I feel it," Nadia says, her eyes pinned to Carmine's back. "We're missing something here. There's a hole in all of this, and I don't like it."

I check my earpiece and hear Uncle Igor in my ear when he says, "They're in. Let's go."

Curt's in the lead, with Nadia right behind him, followed by Maceo, Uncle Igor, the Sergis, Ivie, and me. Once we're near the fence line, we web out, ready to neutralize the security and get inside.

We all want answers.

CHAPTER 18

"**R**emember," Pop mutters as we approach the front door, "we're going to make it seem like this is a friendly visit."

"Right." Shane's voice is cool and hard. "I'm sure we look friendly. Their security has already figured out we're here."

"We will be nice until it's time to *not* be nice," Pop replies and presses the doorbell.

"Well, it's about time you got here."

A young guy answers. Looks to be early twenties. Spoiled. Weak.

I could take this kid out with my pinky finger.

"Was traffic bad from the airport or something?" he asks.

"Hello, Mr. Carlito," Pop says. "I'm Carlo Martinelli."

"I know who you are. By all means, come on in. I can't wait to see this show."

Benji steps back and gestures for us to enter.

"Oh, by the way, go ahead and leave your weapons at the door," he adds.

"You're cute," Carmine replies with a toothy grin. "And I don't think so."

We file past Benji, who's lost his cocky smile, and walk into a living room where my father stops cold.

"Hello, Carlo."

"Claudia?" Pop gasps in surprise. I look at Carmine and then narrow my eyes at the woman sitting in a high-backed chair, her dark hair swept back from her face, her legs crossed, her eyes cool and calm. "My God, have they had you here all these years? Held you against your will?"

She cocks her head to the side and then starts laughing as if she just heard the funniest joke of all time.

"Oh, Carlo. Grow the fuck up. Of course, they haven't been holding me against my will." My father stiffens beside me. "Why don't you all sit down? We'll have a nice family reunion. I'll tell you everything. I've been champing at the bit for *years* to tell you all about my adventures down here in Texas."

Out of the corner of my eye, I see Curt slip silently against the wall and give Shane a signal.

All clear.

"Oh, just let your friends come inside, as well. I always did love an audience."

"Wait, there's more?" Benji asks in disgust as the others file in. My heart calms when I see that Annika is unscathed.

Her eyes are haunted, however.

She killed.

She'll never be the same.

"Oh. Well, look at you," Claudia says to Annika. "You look so different with clothes on."

Igor moves up behind Annika, Ivie, and Nadia as I glare at my aunt.

"You were behind the blackmail," I say.

"Rafe," Claudia says with a small smile. "You grew up to be a handsome man. All three of you did. Of course, I blackmailed her. She spread her legs for literally *any* man who asked. The Tarenkovs should know who they have in their family. It's disgraceful. In fact, the Tarenkovs have a lot of bad eggs. It was just so *easy* to lure Alexander away. To get him to start the drug arm of things. He was eager to defy his father. And let's be honest, he flat-out *hated* his pretty little sister. Of course, I can understand sibling rivalry."

Claudia turns to Pop and winks.

"You're going to die today," Igor says coldly. "For what you did to my family and for much more than that. How does it feel to know that your life can now be measured by mere minutes?"

"Oh, please. I'm not dying today. You all might

think that you took out my security outside, but I have plenty more where they came from, don't you worry." She turns to Pop with a smile. "I must say, I have missed you, brother. You've aged well. How is Flavia? Still weak and whiny?"

"Cut the family reunion bullshit and get to it," Carmine says and raises a brow at Benji when the other man steps toward him. "Oh, I dare you."

"Stop with the dramatics," Claudia says impatiently. "Carlo, I'd like to introduce you to your nephew. My son, Benji."

"Your *son?*" Pop demands.

"Yes. My *son*," Claudia replies as the others in the room shuffle around, ready to pounce and kill her. But we don't have all of the information from her yet. The energy in the room is electric, full of hatred and violence. But Claudia is as calm as ever, almost feeding off the attention, smiling at Benji like a proud mother at a high school graduation. "I suppose I really should start at the beginning, shouldn't I? Vinnie was a piece of shit. We all know that. It's not like the world lost a great man the day he died. I hope he's rotting in hell, where he deserves to be. Mom and Daddy made me marry him because he had the right pedigree, but there was literally *no* attraction there. None at all. We couldn't stand each other. We were married in name only.

"A few years after I married him, I met Francisco. Now *that* was the kind of man I wanted. He was kind and gentle. Not nearly as driven as me, but I was able to overlook that all in the name of love. I spent a great deal of time here in Dallas with him."

"Even after you had Elena," Carmine says.

"Elena." Claudia sighs. "I didn't want to have her. I wasn't interested in having a child with Vinnie at all. The sex was appalling. Ugh, just the thought of it turns my stomach. But that asshole just kept pestering me, *nagging* me to produce an heir for him. Then Mom started in, too, and I got pregnant to shut them all up. I thought about getting an abortion, pretending that I'd lost the baby. But then I thought…I'll just go through with it and hire a fucking nanny. Between the nanny and my family, I hardly ever had to see her."

"Should have just aborted her," Benji spouts off, and before anyone can react, Carmine raises his arm and shoots the other man right between the eyes.

Claudia jumps and stares in horror as her son falls to the floor, dead.

But she just keeps speaking as if nothing at all just happened. Like a cold robot.

"I had Vinnie killed in prison. Staged my death and got the fuck out of that rainy, godforsaken city. Ran to Dallas with Francisco. I had Benji about five years after Elena. Carlo, do you remember those two years or so that I was gone so much, and Mom kept calling you, wanting to know where I was?"

"Yes. I remember."

"Well, it's not like I could go to Seattle to see the

family while I was pregnant with another man's child. Even *I* wouldn't do anything so dramatic."

"Because you know Vinnie would have killed you on the spot," Shane says. "He beat the hell out of Elena, almost killed her, just because she wanted to marry her high school sweetheart, and he thought that was an embarrassment to the family. If you'd shown up pregnant, he would have killed you. And you know it."

"Perhaps." Claudia narrows her eyes and then glances at Benji on the floor. "My son was the *true* heir. The *only* heir. And when Francisco died, God rest his soul, I made it my mission to get rid of all of the other families so Benji could rule, and the Carlitos would be the only organized crime family left. He had Carlito *and* Martinelli blood running through him. Who else could be more ideal to run it all?"

"You killed Vinnie and put an innocent man on death row," Pop says, staring at his sister as if she were a stranger.

"Who gives a shit about that?" Claudia demands. "He was a *criminal*. It was so easy to hire the right judge, a *dirty* one, and make sure he took the fall for it. All tidied up with a pretty little bow."

"Everything you are, everything you stand for, is exactly *against* what we're taught, Claudia," Pop says in exasperation. "My God, you're crazy."

"I am *not* crazy. I'm strong. I'm driven. And I know what I want."

"And would you have killed Elena if you'd known where she was?" Carmine asks.

"I looked for that little brat for *years.* Always slipped through my fingers. Then I found out that my mother was behind hiding my daughter from me." She examines her nails. "So, I killed her."

Pop's hands ball into fists. All of us want to pounce on her.

"You killed *my mother,*" Pop says.

"I killed *my* mother," Claudia shoots back, her eyes full of anger now. "A woman who cared more about you and your three little brats than she ever did about me. She loved my *child* more than me. It was sickening how she fawned over all of you. She didn't even like me. She *ignored* me."

"You were never around," Pop points out. "You spent as much time as you could away."

"You bet your ass, I did."

"And who do you expect was supposed to love Elena? To care for her?"

"God, you're slow, Carlo. Try to keep up here, okay? In case you haven't heard a word I've said, I'll say it again. I don't fucking care about that little cunt," Claudia says, leaning forward. "It was *me* who didn't get any love from anyone in that damn house. So, I came here where I was loved. Appreciated. The Carlitos *worshipped* me."

"So, all of this is because you didn't get enough

attention?" Annika asks and sets her hands on her hips. "Really? That's really stupid."

"You'll watch your tone with me if you want to keep that tongue in your pretty little mouth," Claudia replies, her voice full of venom.

"You just try to touch her," I suggest. "I beg you."

"You blamed my family for protecting Pavlov," Mick Sergi says coldly, now that the Martinelli side of things has been explained. "Built an entire web of lies that my men believed and had dozens of them killed because they believed they were carrying out *my* orders."

"You might want to hire men who aren't so gullible," Claudia says with a shrug. "It's certainly not my fault that they believed a bunch of lies. Besides, it was for the greater good, Mick. Pavlov was a *mess.* And he was from your city. Why didn't you take care of him when he lived there?"

"Because I had him under control," Mick replies. "And then, suddenly, one day he was gone. I thought he was dead and forgot him. Until my men started disappearing and ended up dead, and it all came back to *me.*"

"Well, I had to blame someone for it, didn't I?" Claudia asks. "I mean, I was building an empire for my son."

"And you killed my father," Maceo says.

"I told you. Benji was the only man who could be the boss. The Carlitos are the only family who matter."

"You killed my father and other families who never

had a beef with you," Maceo continues. "My mother could still die."

"You're not *listening* to me." Claudia's frustrated now. "No one else matters except Benji."

"But it was just you and Benji. There is no *Carlito* family," I point out.

"He would have married within a few years and started a family. We would have built from the ground up. But now you've ruined that. You've ruined everything. I should have known you would. The people I came from never did anything good for me, not once in my life. Benji was going to do great things. He had his whole life ahead of him. I just had to get a few roadblocks out of the way, and the sky was the limit for him."

"By killing off the other families," Igor says, shaking his head.

"Yes. You and Nadia were next, but I couldn't pin you down. I was just going to blow you all up."

"And us?" Pop asks.

"I was saving you for last." She taps her lips thoughtfully. "I planned to put the bullets into your heads personally."

"Are you finished with your story?" Pop asks.

Claudia lets out a loud, gusty sigh. "Boy, it feels good to get it all off my chest, you know? Keeping secrets is tough. Yeah, I think that's it for now."

Without another word, Pop raises his gun.

"It's *my* bullet going in *your* head." He squeezes the

trigger and kills her instantly with a bullet right between the eyes.

"Is more security on the way?" I ask Curt, who stayed on the perimeter, keeping an eye out.

"No, we got them all. She may have had more men in different locations, but I disabled the communication systems before we got here."

"We make a pact, here and now," Mick says, his eyes hard and on Claudia as she bleeds from the forehead in her fancy chair. "Nothing like this happens again. We don't let it get this far just because we're too proud to speak to each other. No matter what our issues are."

"Agreed," Igor says with a tired sigh as he looks at Nadia and then the rest of us. "You young people remember this. Let it be a lesson to you. When Mick, Carlo, and I are long gone, and you're the ones in charge, don't let anything like this happen again."

"We won't," Carmine says. "It won't be repeated."

"All because she didn't get enough attention," Annika says again. "I'm no psychiatrist, but I'd say that's psychotic behavior."

"Claudia always had mental health issues," Pop says. "But it sounds like it festered as she got older. I don't know that woman. And now that my family, *all* the families, are safe from her, I'm ready to go home and forget her."

"We have to tell Elena," I remind him. "She deserves to know."

"You're right." Pop pats me on the shoulder as we

file out of the Carlito house. "We'll tell her together. She'll need all of us with her."

"I have a question," Maceo says, catching all of our attention. "Does this mean we're...*friends?*"

"Think of it like this," Mick says thoughtfully. "We've been through a war together. We fought for the same side. We won't always agree and will likely lose touch after this, but in this matter, we're comrades. I'm sorry you lost your father. I liked him very much."

"He didn't die," Maceo says, surprising all of us. "He's also in the ICU. We told everyone he died, so the heat was off him, and I could take care of this."

"Smart." Carmine nods, his face full of admiration for the other underboss. "You're damn smart."

"And we are not your enemy," Maceo says. "None of you. If you ever need us, you know how to find us. Now, I need to get back to my family."

"Let's go home," Annika says, taking my hand in hers.

CHAPTER 19

~RAFE~

*W*e went to her.

Pop would usually ask us to come to him. To meet at his home or his office. But for this, he insisted that we go to Elena's house on the coast of Oregon where she's been staying with her husband, Archer Montgomery.

Carmine called her this morning to let her know we'd be here today, but he didn't give her any other information.

What we have to tell her needs to be done in person. We left the girls in Seattle at Gram's house.

Just as the four of us climb out of the SUV in Elena's driveway, the front door opens, and Archer and Elena come out to greet us.

Elena immediately hugs Pop and then each of us.

"It's really good to see you," she says. "It's been too long."

"You're right," Pop says. "We need to get together more often. We'll start making that happen. Now, let's get in out of this wet."

"Come on in," Archer says with a smile and leads us into a beautiful home set on the cliffs of the Pacific Ocean. "Can I get you anything?"

"Coffee would be great," Pop says. "I take it black."

"Coming right up."

Pop wanders to the windows to watch the storm rage over the water. It's been a harrowing twenty-four hours for him. My father can be a ruthless, cold man. But he loves family more than anything.

He loved his sister.

The woman he remembered her to be all those years ago anyway.

And despite all of the hard things he's done in his life, I know that killing her will be the thing that haunts him for the rest of his days.

"Here we go," Elena says as she and Archer bring trays of coffee with cream and sweetener for anyone who wants it. Once we're all seated in the living room, Elena smiles at all of us, takes a deep breath, and grabs Archer's hand. "You must have news for me. You didn't come all this way just to tell me there's nothing new."

"We do have some things to say," Pop says and takes a sip of coffee, then sets the mug down. "First, I need to apologize to you."

We all look over at him in surprise.

"For what?" Elena asks.

"I knew where you were hiding all of these years. I didn't question your grandmother about her motives. I didn't dig into the situation. I knew you were safe, so I let you live your life. But I did you a disservice. I hurt my entire family."

He shakes his head and stands to pace the room. Pop always did think better when he was on the move.

"Uncle Carlo, you did what you thought was right."

"I did what was easy," he disagrees with an impatient swipe of his arm. "I had three sons to see to and a family to take over. My sister and her husband were dead. But none of that is an excuse."

He turns to Elena and cups her face in his hand. "You very well might hate me after I tell you what I have to tell you."

"I won't hate you," she promises and presses her hand against his. "You can tell me."

I can count on two fingers the number of times I've seen my father look so sad. One was the day my grandmother died.

The other is right now.

"Until yesterday, your mother was very much alive."

Elena gasps and listens intently as Pop relays the entire story from start to finish. He doesn't leave anything out. He doesn't try to spare her from any of the details.

Except for the part when Claudia called Elena a cunt. He keeps that to himself.

"She would have killed me," Elena says as Archer

rubs circles over her back. "I always knew that she didn't like me. She didn't care enough about me to be *mean* to me. She just ignored me. And I was so used to it, I didn't really care. I had good nannies, and I always had all of you."

She stands to pace the room. She always did remind me of my father.

"Should I have known, somewhere deep down, that she was still alive?"

"Why would you?" Carmine asks.

"She was my *mother*," Elena says. "Then again, I never felt a connection to her, so I guess I wouldn't have known. My father was evil. She did the world a favor by having him killed, but my God, Uncle Carlo, an innocent man has been in prison for *years* for something he didn't do."

"I already have his release in motion," Pop says. "He'll be set free soon."

"How did you manage that so quickly?" Shane asks. But Pop just winks at my brother.

"I have connections, son." He turns back to Elena. "And Danvers will be taken care of for the rest of his life. That's a wrong that we can correct."

"Good. That's good." Elena looks out at the storm and then back at Pop. "She killed Gram?"

"Yes, honey."

"I thought Gram died of natural causes?" Carmine asks. "I sat at her bedside. It wasn't a quick death."

"Poison," Shane says shortly. "She made Gram suffer."

"I want to kill that bitch all over again," I say and push my hand through my hair. "She lived too long. She was *happy* for far too long."

"I won't disagree," Elena says. "I also can't believe that I had a half-brother from the time I was five. That's unbelievable."

"I think all of this is pretty unbelievable," Archer says. "It's like something from one of Luke's movies."

"I wish it was fiction," I reply. "I wish you'd known our grandmother. She would have liked you."

"Are we going to bury Claudia?" Elena asks, not referring to the woman as her mother.

"No," Pop says. "Absolutely not. We left her for the cleanup crew. The entire house was burned to the ground with her and that little piece of garbage son she loved so much inside. She doesn't deserve to be buried alongside my parents. I won't mourn for her a second time."

"You absolutely shouldn't," Elena says. "I have to say, I'm relieved that the apple fell quite far from that particular tree in this case. I'm nothing like her."

"You're one of *us*," I reply. "You'll always be ours."

"And mine," Archer says with a smile.

"So, it's good that Gram hid me away." Elena sits and hangs her head in her hands. "I always wondered if it was necessary, or if Gram was overreacting. She didn't tell me who she was hiding me *from*, you know?

Just that someone had killed my parents, and she was afraid they'd come for me, too."

Elena's head shoots up, and her eyes go wide.

"Oh, God. Did Gram know that Claudia was behind it all? That Claudia was alive?"

"We don't think so," Shane says. "I thought of that on the plane. We've been through every piece of paper that pertains to the case. More than once. We can't ask her to be certain, but she never mentions in any of her notes that she knew about Claudia. She hired many investigators over the years. If she knew about Claudia, she wouldn't have needed to do that."

"Good." Elena swallows hard as tears fill her beautiful, bi-colored eyes. "Because that would have just tortured her all those years."

"This chapter is now closed," Pop says and reaches for Elena's hand. "There's no need for you to look over your shoulder anymore, Elena. You can truly put it all behind you and live your life as you wish."

"I'm glad. It's a relief. Because I have news, too." She grabs Archer's hand again with her free one. "We're going to have a baby. And it's going to be born into peace. And love."

"Ah, little one." Pop gathers Elena close and kisses the top of her head. "This might be the most loved baby to ever be conceived. I can't wait to meet him or her."

"Can they call you Papa?" Elena asks. "You're the only father I've ever known."

For the first time in my life, I see my father's eyes fill with tears. "It would be my honor."

"DO YOU HEAR THAT?" Annika asks, making me stop on the path that runs through my grandmother's estate.

I stop and listen. "No. What?"

"Quiet." She smiles and tips her face up to the sunshine. "It's so quiet. And the air is light, like a huge weight has been lifted."

"Because it has." I kiss her hand, and we begin walking again, headed toward the pond where I spent summers splashing and swimming. Making mischief.

It's here, in this special place, that I want to do what I'm about to do.

I'm not even nervous.

Okay, I'm a *little* nervous.

When we reach the bench by the water and Annika sits down, I lower myself to one knee and smile up at the most beautiful woman in the world.

Every time I look at her, my breath catches.

"Rafe."

"Annika." I grin and reach into my pocket for the ring. No box, just a ring. When I take her hand in mine, I'm surprised to find it shaking. "I'm supposed to be the nervous one."

She just laughs and swipes at a tear on her cheek.

"I feel like this is millennia in the making. It seems

like I've wanted to ask you this question for all of my adult life. And I know that there were reasons before why it wasn't possible for us to be together.

"Those reasons are gone now. And I know that if I don't ask you to be mine, as soon as humanly possible, I'll regret it. I don't want to waste any more time, Annika. You're my soul mate. I need to be with you the way I need air. And I know what you're going to say."

She just laughs and swipes at more tears.

"You're going to say that we're together. And we are. It's awesome. But I want more. I want *everything*. I want to make it legal. I want to give you my name. I want the whole package."

"You want a lot."

I sigh and lean in to kiss her cheek. "Yeah. I want a lot. But I'll give you back just as much, if not more."

"I know you will."

"Is that a yes?"

"You didn't actually ask me anything yet."

"Oh. Right." I clear my throat. "Will you marry me?"

"Of course." She flings her arms around my shoulders and buries that sweet face in my neck. "Of course, I will, Rafe. There's nothing in the world that I want more."

"Thank God." I ease back so I can slip the ring onto her finger.

"Oh, this is *stunning*. And so unique."

"Yeah." I kiss the ring on her finger and then slide up onto the bench with her. "The big diamond in the middle was my gram's. Not from her wedding ring. My mom has that. But it was from a ring that my grandfather gave her on their twenty-fifth anniversary. She loved it very much. The green stone is from my mom."

Her blue eyes fly to mine in surprise.

"Yeah, I asked her for help on this because I didn't want to screw it up. Anyway, the emerald is from a necklace my father gave her for a birthday gift. The ruby is from *your* mom."

"The ring my father gave her when she had me," Annika says softly. "I've always admired that ring."

"That's what she said. The sapphires are from your Aunt Katya. They were earrings gifted to her by Igor."

"Rafe, this is amazing."

"One more thing," I reply. "The gold is from Ivie. It was her mother's wedding band."

Annika gasps and starts to cry again. "*Rafe.*"

"The ring is all of us, Annika. Because family is important, and they're all a part of us. They support us. They love us. And it's with huge relief that I say I asked your father *and* Igor if I could ask for your hand, and they both gave me their blessing."

She laughs as she turns her face up to me. "Well, I would have been surprised if they'd said no."

"Still, I was nervous as hell."

She sighs and settles in next to me on the bench as we quietly watch the water for a long moment. Ducks splash, but the leaves have long fallen, and winter is on the way.

"I have something else to discuss with you," I say.

"You're full of news today."

I shrug and tighten the arm I have slung around her shoulders.

"Yeah, well, I've been doing a lot of thinking. And I had a long talk with my father last night after you went to bed. I know you like it here in Seattle, but what do you think about this specific place?"

"Your grandmother's house?"

"Yes. We need a house. More space. The condo just won't do forever. And last night, while talking with Pop, I brought up the idea of you and I living here. It's been sitting empty since Gram died. We've used it as a home base these past few weeks, but for the most part, it's just sat. This house needs a family in it. And Pop agrees that, if you don't hate the idea, we would be good here."

"I have so many questions," she whispers.

"You hate the idea."

"No. Not at all. But, Rafe, this is a *huge* house for just us."

"It's big," I agree. "I can't change the size of it. We have caretakers for the grounds, and housekeepers for inside. Also, Pop's fine with us changing anything we want. He just asked that if we want to rehome some of the art, that we give it to him to see to."

"I'd like to change a few things, but it's really beautiful the way it is."

I look down at her. "Is that a yes?"

"Your brothers and Elena are okay with it?"

"Yes. I've spoken with them, as well. It's not leaving the family. And they're always welcome here. The thing is, I like the idea of *our* home being the anchor, you know? A place where the family can always come to gather together. Holidays, special events, that sort of thing. Gram would love that."

"I love that, too. I've been so at home here. I think making this our place is a good idea. Because I have something to tell you, too."

I raise a brow, waiting.

"We're going to start filling those extra bedrooms upstairs sooner than we expected."

"Are you telling me—?"

"I'm pregnant." She grins, and when I let out a whoop and spin her in the air, she laughs loudly. "Put me down before you make me throw up."

"Are you okay? Do you feel all right? Do you need anything?"

"I'm great." She cradles my face in her hands. "And I have everything I need right here."

"Let's go tell everyone all the things."

I take her hand and lead her back to the house.

"You mean they don't already know?"

"They don't know everything. Let's go share this with them."

"Good idea."

EPILOGUE

~CARLO MARTINELLI~

One Month Later

"We did it." I light my cigar and smile over at my friend as we survey the room. We're in the ballroom of my mother's home, Rocco's home now, watching the party unfold around us, celebrating the wedding of my youngest son and his darling Annika. "We managed to match them all together."

Igor grins and sips his whiskey. Our table is on the edge of the room where we can keep watch over our two families. Our wives are huddled together. And the kids are dancing, laughing, and enjoying each other.

"A good-looking bunch, our young ones," Igor says with a salute of his glass. "Smart. Strong."

"And powerful."

We share a pleased look.

We achieved what my sister longed for all along. We managed to build the strongest organized crime family in the country.

I feel the familiar pang in my chest that always comes when I think of my sister. I wish things had been different.

But they aren't. And that chapter is closed.

The new one ahead looks like the beginning of a bright future for our children and our grandchildren.

"They take after us," Igor says and clinks his glass to mine. "Do you think they have any idea that we put their matches into motion?"

"Of course, not." I sip my whiskey and then puff the cigar. "They're smart, but we were cunning. Had some surprises and bumps along the way."

"But we got here all the same," Igor replies. "And that's the important thing. My firefly is happy with your Rocco."

I gaze across the room where Rocco lifts Annika into his arms and kisses her soundly. There is nothing I love more than my family.

"It's been a long time coming."

"Unfortunate, but necessary," he says. "And I believe they'll be all the stronger because of it."

"Agreed. They'll give us beautiful babies."

"Indeed, they will. Thank you for offering them this home."

"I was surprised when Rocco asked me for it, but it made sense. He's always been more rooted here than my other children. It's the right thing to do. And I know that he and Annika will always open their doors to you and your family, just as they will to me and mine."

"We are one family now," Igor says. "Twenty years ago, I would have thought it impossible."

"And now?"

"I'm grateful."

"As am I, my friend."

We puff our cigars and watch our brood, and I know, without a doubt, that our family is safe, ready for future generations of Martinellis and Tarenkovs to rule.

Our families will go on.

And that, is the ultimate goal.

I HOPE you enjoyed my mafia family! If you haven't read the book where it all began, You Belong With Me, you can get it now! Elena and Archer's story is here:

https://www.kristenprobyauthor.com/you-belong-with-me

AND, keep reading for a look at You Belong With Me!

YOU BELONG WITH ME

A WITH ME IN SEATTLE NOVEL

You Belong With Me
A With Me In Seattle Novel
By
Kristen Proby

YOU BELONG WITH ME

A With Me In Seattle Novel

Kristen Proby

Copyright © 2020 by Kristen Proby

All Rights Reserved. This book may not be reproduced, scanned, or distributed in any printed or electronic form without permission from the author. Please do not participate in or encourage piracy of copyrighted materials in violation of the author's rights. All characters and storylines are the property of the author and your support and respect are appreciated. The characters and events portrayed in this book are fictitious. Any similarity to real persons, living or dead, is coincidental and not intended by the author.

Cover Design: By Hang Le

Cover photo: Eric Battershell Photography

Published by Ampersand Publishing, Inc.

This book is for Rachel Van Dyken, without whom it may not have come to fruition.
Thank you for your encouragement, and your friendship.
I love you.

PROLOGUE

Twelve Years Ago
~Elena~

$\mathcal{I}$'ve always hated this room. My father's office is grand, full of honey oak bookcases, a massive chandelier, and a desk in the center of the space that's bigger than the bed I sleep on. Floor-to-ceiling windows are at his back and look out over the estate that he insisted on but, in large part, ignores.

Whenever I'm due for a massive lecture, this is where he drags me.

"May I please speak with you?"

"What is it?" He doesn't look up from his computer, which doesn't surprise me. Paying attention to his daughter has never been a priority for this man. I'll just share my news and go straight to my room, pack my things, and be out of here for good.

I can almost *smell* the freedom. I can't wait to move in with my husband. *My husband.* That word makes me want to spin in circles of excitement. Archer and I will make a home and have babies. His family is wonderful, and there will be so much love in our household. Our kids will never question whether we love them. They'll never be afraid. And when the time comes, they'll be able to marry whomever they please.

"I got married." I square my shoulders and lift my chin. "Three days ago."

I'm not afraid of my father. Not now. But my stomach quivers with butterflies. I'm eighteen years old. An adult. And I'm able to make my own decisions without influence from my parents.

What can he do? What's done is done.

He looks up from his desk, and his cold eyes narrow.

"And who, exactly, did you marry, Elena?"

"Archer Montgomery."

He sets his pen aside and leans back in his big, black chair, silently watching me. His calculating stare makes me want to squirm, but I hold steady.

"Isn't that the boy I told you to stop seeing a year ago?"

"He's a good man, Dad. If you'd just give him a chance—"

He stands and paces behind the desk, looking out the windows and shoving his hands into his pockets.

Maybe he'll just tell me to leave. That would be the best-case scenario.

"What is your last name, Elena?"

"Montgomery."

"Don't." His voice isn't loud, but it's firm.

"Watkins."

He turns and stares at me impassively. "That's right. And that last name, along with the Martinellis', holds more weight than you can ever fully understand. It means that, as my daughter, you don't have the freedom to marry whomever you choose, whenever you decide to do it."

"I'm an adult."

"You're *my daughter*!"

I blink at the spurt of anger. He's not impassive now. His eyes shoot daggers at me, and sweat breaks out across my skin.

"Dad, I love him."

He shakes his head and waves off my comment as if it's an annoying fly buzzing around his head.

"We'll have it annulled immediately."

"No."

He lifts an eyebrow. I've *never* told my father no. I don't think anyone in his life ever has.

No one would dare.

"Excuse me?"

I lift my chin again. "No."

He stalks around his desk and grips my arm just above my elbow, almost painfully, and drags me through the house, up the stairs, and into my bedroom.

"You're putting me in time out?"

"I should have done this a long time ago. You're too spoiled. Too indulged. You think you can defy me, go against what's best for the family like this?" We keep moving quickly through the room to my closet, where he pulls a sash off my robe, yanks my arms above my head, and ties me to the light fixture in the middle of the room. He steps back, barely breathing hard. "This is where you'll stay until you come to your senses."

And then he walks out.

"Wake up."

I open my eyes and moan in pain. My shoulders are screaming. My hands are numb.

"Uncomfortable?" my father asks.

I don't reply.

"Was sixteen hours enough time for you to reevaluate your decisions?"

"Dad." I lick my lips. My voice isn't whiny. I'm not a little girl begging for a pony. I'm a grown woman, trying to reason with another adult. "What's done is done. We're married. We love each other. I didn't do anything to hurt anyone, and I didn't want to defy you. If you'd just give him a chance, I know you'd like him."

"It's not about *liking* him, daughter." He sits on my bench. He's in his usual uniform of slacks, a dress shirt, and a tie. He wears this every day of his life. "You're betrothed to Alexander Tarenkov. You've known that since you were twelve."

"I've never met that man in my life."

"It doesn't matter."

"This is ridiculous. I'm not marrying a stranger. This is the twenty-first century. Women can marry who they want."

"Not mafia women."

"I didn't choose this."

"It's a privilege," he insists. "You were blessed with this by birthright, whether you like it or not."

"I'm not divorcing Archer. I'm not giving him up, no matter what you say." I'm breathing hard now. The tears want to come, but I will them back. Just the thought of losing Archer sends searing pain through my heart. I can't live without him.

I won't.

"You'll do as you're told."

"No."

"There's that word again." There's an edge to his voice now. One I haven't heard before. "I'm not fond of it."

"Well, get used to it."

"I didn't raise you to be disrespectful to your father."

"You *didn't raise me*. Grandma did. Nannies did. Not

you. And certainly not that pitiful excuse for a woman who gave birth to me."

He stands and walks to me. His face is inches from mine, and I can smell the coffee on his breath.

"You will watch your tongue."

"Or what?"

He rears his hand back as if he's going to slap me, but I stare him in the eye and tilt my head.

"You won't hurt me. The mafia doesn't hurt their women, remember?"

But he does. He follows through and slaps me across the face. The coppery taste of blood fills my mouth.

"I'm not just your father," he says calmly as he walks away and sets a briefcase I didn't see earlier on the bench. He snaps it open. "I'm a mob boss. I'm the one who protects the family, who oversees *everything*. Did you think I didn't know about you and Archer?"

My stomach jumps, but I don't reply.

I watch as my father unbuttons the sleeves of his shirt and rolls them up to his elbows. He unfastens the top button of his collar and then loosens his tie before taking it off.

He removes his Rolex and sets it aside, and then pulls his long, salt-and-pepper hair back at the nape of his neck.

"I know every move you make, daughter." He glances over his shoulder at me. "I gave you some slack to have your little romance. It kept you occupied, and you're right, Archer comes from a good family. You were safe.

"But to have the audacity to run off and get *married* when you knew it would be forbidden? That, I can't forgive. I've been too soft on you. The annulment is already in the works."

"I won't sign it."

He laughs now. "Do you think I need you to sign it? Elena, you disappoint me."

"I'll just marry him again. You can't keep us apart."

He sighs and reaches into the briefcase and pulls out a whip. It's long and well-worn.

"Dad."

He circles the room, walking around me. He rips my T-shirt in two, exposing my back, then returns to dragging the whip, flicking it with his wrist as if he's warming up.

He's just scaring me.

I'm so sick of this shit! Just let me leave so I can be with Archer!

He walks behind me, and to my utter shock and horror, he cracks that whip across my back, sending crazy, searing pain throughout my body.

"That's one," he says, his voice as calm and cool as glass.

I can't believe it. He *hurt* me.

"What's best for the family is always the priority," he

says and lashes the whip over my back again, making me cry out in pain this time. "You know this. You *know.*"

"I love him," I whisper, and am rewarded with another lash of the whip.

"Do you think I give a fuck?"

More lashes. He counts ten, then pauses and punches my face. I see stars when he hits me square on the nose, and then he picks the whip back up and counts another ten lashes. And when he's done, and I can no longer cry or speak, he simply rolls up the whip and tucks it into his briefcase.

I can't stand anymore. I'm hanging by my useless, dead hands. I can feel the warm blood trickling down my back, soaking my shorts. Blood also runs down my face, and my eyes are swollen.

"It looks like you need more time to think." His voice is calm again. His impassive eyes roam over my face before he turns and walks out, leaving me alone once more.

THE LIGHTS COME ON, blinding me.

"The annulment is complete."

My back sings in pain, as does my face. I have a headache the size of Texas. I can't see well.

But I'm going to live through this, and then I'm

going to leave. I'm going to run away with Archer. We can live *anywhere.*

"I can get married again."

"Tsk tsk." He sets a laptop on the bench and opens it, then taps some keys. Suddenly, a video of Archer fills the screen. "Looks like he's having lunch with his sister."

Archer and Anastasia.

"This is live," Dad continues as if we're having a conversation about the weather. "Oh, see this man here?"

He points to the corner of the screen where a man I recognize as one of my father's goons sits at a table nearby.

"He's armed and has been given the command to kill them both when they leave this restaurant if you don't make the right decision. Right here, right now."

My eyes fly to his in shock.

"You wouldn't *kill* him." My voice is like sandpaper.

"You underestimate me, little girl. Even after the beating I handed out last night, you still underestimate me. Did you think I'd let you walk out of here and go off with him? Or let you sneak away?"

I can't reply. My eyes are on the man I love as he laughs with Anastasia. Oh, how I wish I was with them.

"I can't believe you're doing this."

"You have two choices. Either he dies, or you do what you were born to do and think of what's best for your family."

Archer is my family!

"Either way," he continues, "you won't be with him. You just need to decide if he lives or dies."

"This is so fucked-up."

"Quite," he agrees. And when I look into his eyes, I can see that he's enjoying himself.

He *wants* to hurt me.

He's getting off on it.

And I don't doubt that he'd kill Archer just to fuck with my head.

"Fine." I lick my bloody lip and feel everything inside myself break. I feel my heart die. How will I go on without Archer? How will I live for the rest of my life without him in it? But Archer losing his life isn't an option. I *have* to keep him safe. "You win."

"There." Father closes the laptop with a satisfied snap. "That wasn't so hard, was it?"

I expect him to untie me, but he turns away and picks up a lighter and lets the flame lick the big ring he wears with a prominent *W* on it. He doesn't wear a wedding band, but he's worn that stupid, gaudy ring every day of his life.

I want to shove it down his throat and let him choke on it.

"And this is so you always remember who it is that you belong to."

Before I can do anything, he presses the hot metal to my skin, high on my thigh, and I scream in pain as he brands me.

He fucking branded me!

I want to claw out his eyes. I want to spit in his face. But I go limp as a rag and wait as he unties my hands and helps me fall to a heap on the floor.

"I'll send a nurse up to tend to those wounds," he says. "And, Elena, if I find out that you have any words with Archer aside from breaking it off, or if you try to see him, I *will* kill him."

I watch his feet as he walks out of my closet, and then I curl in on myself, crying harder than I ever have in my life. Not from the open wounds on my back, or the burning flesh on my thigh.

No, the pain of losing Archer forever is far worse than any physical pain could ever be.

"Hey."

I'm holding the phone close to my ear, eager to soak in every word we say, even though they're going to be painful. He's going to hate me before this call is over.

"Where the hell are you, E? I haven't heard from you in *days*. A man shouldn't go that long without talking to his wife, you know?"

I close my eyes. *Wife.* Oh, how I long to be his spouse. To truly be his until the end of time.

"Yeah, we need to talk about that, Archer. We were really impulsive."

"Planned it for three months," he reminds me. "I don't think that's impulsive."

"Well, it was for me. You know, I think I just got really caught up in the idea of getting married and everything, but now that I've had time to think it over, I don't think this is what I want at all."

He's quiet for a moment. I want to scream, *I'M LYING! HE'S MAKING ME DO THIS TO US!*

But I can't.

"What are you saying, E? Do you want to go back to dating?"

"No." I swallow hard and hate myself for what I'm about to say. "No, I think it's best if we just go ahead and part ways now. Clean break. I'm sorry if I hurt you, Archer, but it's really what I want."

"I can't believe this."

I have to push my hand against my sore mouth so I don't sob out loud.

"You're *breaking up* with me?"

"Yeah. I'm just too young to be tied down, you know? I need to experience life and spend some time alone. You're just not what I want, Archer."

"But we're married." I can hear him pacing on the other end of the line.

"It can be annulled." Even the word tastes bitter in my mouth. It's the last thing I want, but my father was right. Neither of us needs to sign anything for the mob boss of the Watkins family to make it happen.

There's a beat of silence and then he hangs up

without saying goodbye. I've just broken his heart, and I hate myself for it.

I hate my family. My father especially.

Rage flows through me, swift and hot. When it burns out, I feel...nothing. I'll never let anyone hurt me like this again.

CHAPTER 1

~ELENA~

Beep! Beep! Beep!

I roll over and kill the alarm. I've been awake for at least an hour already, lying in my warm, cozy bed, watching the sky turn from black to purple to blue. I've always been an early riser, which is why my job is so perfect for me.

Baby animals need their breakfast, and at the Oregon Coast Wild Animal Rescue, I'm the lucky woman who gets to feed them.

I stretch my arms over my head and then sit up, letting the blankets fall around my hips, exposing my naked body to the crisp morning air.

Summer is waning, and it won't be long before I have to turn on the heat. But I've been clinging to the season with all of my might. Once winter arrives, we'll have more rain and grey days than I care to think about. So, I plan to hold on to these nice summer moments for as long as I can.

I throw a robe around my shoulders, slide my feet into slippers, and pad downstairs to my small kitchen.

I live in what I lovingly refer to as a cottage. That's probably too grand a word for my little cabin in Oregon. My bedroom is a loft upstairs, and down below, I only have a kitchen, a small living space, and an efficient bathroom.

But it's only me here, so it fits me just fine. In the six years that I've lived in Bandon, Oregon, I've never needed more than this.

I come from mansions and a life of privilege, yet nothing has ever made me feel as safe as this.

I pop a pod in my Keurig, set my *Blow me, I'm hot* mug on the counter, and as my first cup of coffee brews, I step out onto the deck that gives me just a tiny peek at the ocean. The sky is clear today, and the wind is calmer than usual, so I make a mental note and promise myself I'll take a walk on the beach this after-noon after work and lunch with my friend, Lindsey.

With another deep breath, I turn back inside and pour some cream into my coffee, then carry it with me into the living room.

This is my typical morning routine, seven days a week, whether rain or shine. I sit on a small pillow in the corner of the room, crisscross applesauce, close my eyes, and begin my meditation.

I go to my happy place in my mind.

It's on a boat at a marina in Seattle with Archer. Even after all these years, following drama and hurt and more shit than I care to dwell on, it's always Archer I think about when I go to my happy place.

His smile. His gentle hands. Archer was my safe place, my constant source of stability in a life that was anything *but* stable.

When you're the daughter of a mob boss, life is damn scary.

Three minutes later, with a clear mind and relaxed shoulders, I retrieve my coffee and go about the rest of my routine. Shower. Makeup. Hair up in a ponytail.

When I'm dressed and have another cup of coffee in my trusty *Girls rule!* to-go mug, I set off for work in my old, rusted-out Buick. Saying it's second-hand is too kind. It was most likely fifth-hand.

But it does the job and gets me to and from just fine.

It also doesn't draw any unwanted attention.

It's a ten-minute drive to the rescue. I park in my usual spot and walk into the nursery, which is dimly lit as soft music plays through Bluetooth speakers.

It feels like a spa. Like someone's going to hand me a robe and a cup of tea and lead me back to a massage room.

But instead, we have mountain lion cubs, raccoon kits, and a baby sloth, all waiting for my attention.

"Hey, Ally."

I smile, used to being called Ally now. I changed my

name when I moved to Bandon, complete with a credit history, passport, and driver's license. All after I spent two years in California under a different name. Unfortunately, I ran into a school friend unexpectedly at the vineyard that I worked at and had to run again.

The mob has connections for a girl who needs to disappear.

"Good morning, Chad." I smile at the man, who's feeding one of the mountain lion cubs with a bottle. "How did it go last night?"

"Pretty normal," he says. "Cleaned up a bunch of poop and fed roughly four hundred bottles."

I laugh at the exaggeration, although there have been times when it felt like that many.

"Is everyone healthy?"

"Raccoon kit red didn't want to eat," he says with a frown, nodding at the pen behind me. "Keep an eye on her."

"Will do. Thanks."

We tie strings of different colors around the animals' necks so we can tell them apart from each other and keep accurate records on each one.

I love this job. It's exactly what I always wanted to do, even when I was a little girl. I'm fiercely protective of it, and I don't even care that I work six hours a day, seven days a week since we lost an employee last year and haven't replaced her.

This is where I'm needed, and I love it.

Really. I do.

NEWSLETTER SIGN UP

I hope you enjoyed reading this story as much as I enjoyed writing it! For upcoming book news, be sure to join my newsletter! I promise I will only send you news-filled mail, and none of the spam. You can sign up here:

https://mailchi.mp/kristenproby.com/
newsletter-sign-up

ALSO BY KRISTEN PROBY:

Other Books by Kristen Proby

The With Me In Seattle Series

Come Away With Me
Under The Mistletoe With Me
Fight With Me
Play With Me
Rock With Me
Safe With Me
Tied With Me
Breathe With Me
Forever With Me
Stay With Me
Indulge With Me
Love With Me
Dance With Me

ALSO BY KRISTEN PROBY:

Dream With Me
You Belong With Me
Imagine With Me
Shine With Me
Escape With Me

Check out the full series here: https://www.
kristenprobyauthor.com/with-me-in-seattle

The Big Sky Universe

Love Under the Big Sky
Loving Cara
Seducing Lauren
Falling for Jillian
Saving Grace

The Big Sky
Charming Hannah
Kissing Jenna
Waiting for Willa
Soaring With Fallon

Big Sky Royal
Enchanting Sebastian
Enticing Liam
Taunting Callum

Heroes of Big Sky

Honor

Courage

Check out the full Big Sky universe here: https://www.kristenprobyauthor.com/under-the-big-sky

Bayou Magic

Shadows

Spells

Check out the full series here: https://www.kristenprobyauthor.com/bayou-magic

The Romancing Manhattan Series

All the Way

All it Takes

After All

Check out the full series here: https://www.kristenprobyauthor.com/romancing-manhattan

The Boudreaux Series

Easy Love

Easy Charm

Easy Melody

Easy Kisses

Easy Magic

Easy Fortune

Easy Nights

Check out the full series here: https://www.
kristenprobyauthor.com/boudreaux

The Fusion Series

Listen to Me

Close to You

Blush for Me

The Beauty of Us

Savor You

Check out the full series here: https://www.
kristenprobyauthor.com/fusion

From 1001 Dark Nights

Easy With You

Easy For Keeps

No Reservations

Tempting Brooke

Wonder With Me

Shine With Me

Kristen Proby's Crossover Collection

Soaring with Fallon, A Big Sky Novel

Wicked Force: A Wicked Horse Vegas/Big Sky Novella
By Sawyer Bennett

All Stars Fall: A Seaside Pictures/Big Sky Novella
By Rachel Van Dyken

Hold On: A Play On/Big Sky Novella
By Samantha Young

Worth Fighting For: A Warrior Fight Club/Big Sky
Novella
By Laura Kaye

Crazy Imperfect Love: A Dirty Dicks/Big Sky Novella
By K.L. Grayson

Nothing Without You: A Forever Yours/Big Sky
Novella
By Monica Murphy

Check out the entire Crossover Collection here:
https://www.kristenprobyauthor.com/kristen-proby-
crossover-collection

ABOUT THE AUTHOR

Kristen Proby has published close to sixty titles, many of which have hit the USA Today, New York Times and Wall Street Journal Bestsellers lists. She continues to self publish, best known for her With Me In Seattle, Big Sky and Boudreaux series.

Kristen and her husband, John, make their home in her hometown of Whitefish, Montana with their two cats and French Bulldog named Rosie.

facebook.com/booksbykristenproby
instagram.com/kristenproby
bookbub.com/profile/kristen-proby
goodreads.com/kristenproby